2 Quiz #-109205
L-4.8
AR pts-5.0

WHO WON THE WAR?

■　■　■　■　■　■

■ ■ ■ ■ ■ ■ ■ ■ ■

WHO WON THE WAR?

■

Phyllis Reynolds Naylor

DELACORTE PRESS

Published by
Delacorte Press
an imprint of
Random House Children's Books
a division of Random House, Inc.
New York

Visit us on the Web! www.randomhouse.com/kids
Educators and librarians, for a variety of teaching tools, visit
us at www.randomhouse.com/teachers

Library of Congress Cataloging-in-Publication Data
Naylor, Phyllis Reynolds.
Who won the war? / Phyllis Reynolds Naylor.
p.   cm.
Summary: As the end of summer approaches, the Malloy girls decide they will
really try to get along with the Hatford boys before moving back to Ohio,
but after all the practical jokes and competitions of the previous year,
the boys just do not trust the girls.
ISBN-10: 0-385-73141-8 (trade)—ISBN-10: 0-385-90172-0 (glb.)
ISBN-13: 978-0-385-73141-6 (trade)—ISBN-13: 978-0-385-90172-7 (glb.)
[1. Brothers—Fiction.   2. Sisters—Fiction.   3. Neighbors—Fiction.]
I. Title.
PZ7.N24Wjo 2006
[Fic]—dc22

2005037067

The text of this book is set in 12-point Adobe Garamond.

Printed in the United States of America

September 2006

10 9 8 7 6 5 4 3 2 1

For my grandson, Garrett Riley Naylor

Contents

■　■　■　■　■　■

■ ■ ■ ■ ■ ■ ■ ■ ■ ■ ■

One

■

The News

It was official: they were going back.

After Mrs. Malloy put down the phone, Caroline sneaked a look at her two older sisters. Was either of them going to cry?

It certainly wouldn't be Eddie, the oldest. Beth? Possible, but not likely. No, if anyone was going to get emotional about leaving Buckman, it would be Caroline herself. She swallowed.

"Well," said their mother. "I guess that's that."

"Goodbye, West Virginia! Hello, Ohio!" said Eddie.

When Mr. Malloy had taken a job at the college in Buckman on a teacher-exchange program, they'd all known that it would only be for a year. He had been offered other jobs too in Buckman, however, and the girls—and even their mother—had wondered if he might decide to stay.

But now he was back in Ohio, he'd signed the job contract, and the Malloys would be moving on August 24. The Bensons, whose house the Malloys had been renting, would be back on August 31.

There was silence around the dinner table. The shrimp salad sat half eaten on their plates, the lemon slices undisturbed in the iced tea.

"Well, at least I get to finish out summer baseball," Eddie said at last. She'd be entering middle school when they got back home.

"I think I'm going to be sad," said Beth, who was a year younger. "I'll miss the library—being able to walk to it, I mean."

"I'll miss the river and the swinging footbridge," said Caroline, age nine. She had a dark ponytail, while her two older sisters were blond.

More silence.

Then Eddie started to grin. "What I *won't* miss . . . ," she began, glancing at the others, and the three girls chimed together, "the *Hatfords*!" They laughed, but Caroline knew it wasn't true. They *would* miss the boys.

"Do you remember the day we moved in here?" Eddie asked her sisters.

"How could we forget?" said Beth. "We caught them up on the roof of their house, watching us from across the river."

"And they dumped dead birds and squirrels on our side to make us think the river was polluted, just so we'd go back to Ohio," said Caroline.

"Why, you never told me that!" said her mother.

"Ha!" said Eddie. "We never told you half the stuff those stupid guys did!"

Caroline knew, of course, that the Hatford brothers—Jake and Josh and Wally and Peter—weren't stupid in the least. Annoying, disgusting, and conniving, yes, but they had outwitted the girls on several occasions and entertained them on others, and though Eddie might not admit it, the girls had never had so much fun in their lives.

Later that evening, when Mrs. Malloy was packing up books in the living room and the girls were doing the dishes, Eddie said, "You know, if we've got only three more weeks here, we'd better make them count."

"Doing what?" asked Beth.

"Showing the Hatford boys once and for all who's in charge, what else?"

"In charge of what?" asked Caroline. "We're moving back to Ohio. How can we be in charge of anything?"

"In charge of us! In charge of *them*! What I mean is, we have to show them we won."

"I didn't know we were at war," said Beth.

"Of course you did," said Eddie. "War broke out the first day we got here! I just don't want those guys telling the Benson boys that they led us around by the nose all year. That they tricked us so many times we didn't know up from down. We've got to pull a couple more tricks ourselves."

"Maybe we could just do something *fun* with them," said Beth. "We don't have to fight."

"Did I say *fight*?" asked Eddie. "I simply want them to remember that the Malloys are not to be messed with. We'll have fun, all right. Trust me."

Caroline sighed and took the pan Beth handed her, wiped it off, and put it back in the cupboard. Everything was a competition with Eddie—a race, a contest. There had to be winners and losers, first place and second. The champions and the defeated.

All that Caroline, actress-to-be, wanted to do before they left was sneak into the old elementary school auditorium a few more times and act out little scenes up on a real stage. Her elementary school back in Ohio didn't have an auditorium with plush seats for the audience. It didn't have a stage with lights and scenery and a velvet curtain to pull when a performance was over. The only place to put on a production in the school back home was the gym, which also served as a lunchroom and usually smelled of bananas and pizza.

"So," said Beth to Eddie. "What are we going to do?"

Eddie's eyes narrowed. In fact, they almost seemed to glow, Caroline thought. Like a wolf's eyes. Glowing eyes on Eddie were bad news. They meant she was up to something, and whatever it was, Beth and Caroline would get blamed for it too.

"Well, you know how Jake brags about all the wild things they used to do when the Bensons lived here?" Eddie said. "I'll bet they didn't do half the stuff he says they did. Knob Hill, the old Indian burial ground where the spirits roam at night? Ha! 'Okay, Jake, take us there,' I'm going to tell him. The old coal mine? 'Hey, let's go!' Smuggler's Cove? 'I'm up for it!' "

Caroline didn't especially like the sound of roaming spirits or an old coal mine. And the one time they had been to Smuggler's Cove with the boys, she had almost got thrown into the water. But the possibility of Eddie and Beth doing anything without her was unthinkable. So she said what she had to say: "Sure."

"We'll tell Jake to put up or shut up," said Eddie.

"But be nice to Josh," said Beth. "He's not so bad. And Peter's cute. Wally? Wally is just . . ."

"Just Wally," said Caroline.

"Girls," their mother said, coming to the doorway. "Each day from now until the twenty-fourth, I want you to pack at least three things. I've put a box in each of your rooms, and if you pack a little every day, it won't be such a chore at the end."

"If we keep packing stuff, we'll run out of clothes to wear," said Beth. "They'll all be in boxes."

"That's the idea," said Mrs. Malloy. "We want to be ready to go, so that as soon as the movers have loaded our things into the van, we can get in the car and drive off."

The girls trooped upstairs, but instead of sorting through their closets, they sat down on the floor by the window in Caroline's room and gazed out at the river and the house beyond, where the Hatfords lived. The Buckman River flowed into town on one side of Island

Avenue, circled around under the road bridge leading to the business district, and flowed back out again on the other side. It was here that the Malloys lived in the Bensons' house, and a swinging footbridge connected their side of the river to the Hatfords' on College Avenue.

"Do you remember the bottle race we had on the river?" asked Beth.

"Yeah," said Eddie. "And the time the boys brought over that box with the chiffon cake in it? Only we thought it was dead birds or something and threw it in the water?"

Caroline gave a little sigh. "It's going to be boring walking to school on a sidewalk instead of a swinging bridge," she said.

"Oh, for Pete's sake, let's quit moaning," said Eddie. "Let's each throw three things into our packing boxes and then go downstairs and call the Hatfords. I'll do the talking."

She stood up and yanked open one of Caroline's dresser drawers. She pulled out a pack of Uno cards, a necklace, and a pair of underpants and tossed them into the empty box Mrs. Malloy had placed on Caroline's bed.

"Next!" she said, and led them into Beth's room.

There Eddie opened the closet, grabbed a belt, and tossed it into Beth's box. She found a book and a pair of loafers and added those.

"Next!" she crowed. In her own room, she put two pair of socks and a baseball cap into the packing box.

"Done!" she said, and they all marched downstairs and crowded around the phone in the hallway.

As usual, after Eddie dialed, she held the phone slightly away from her ear so that her sisters could hear too.

"Hello?" she said. "Peter?"

Caroline moved in a little closer.

"This is Eddie," her sister said. "How you doing?"

"O-kaaaay!" came Peter's voice, and Caroline and Beth grinned at each other. He was the youngest of the Hatfords, just out of second grade.

"How's your summer going?" asked Eddie.

"Boring," Peter answered.

"Really?" said Eddie. "Well, maybe we can liven it up a little. Is Jake around?"

"No," said Peter.

"What about Josh?"

"He's not here either," said Peter.

"Wally? Where *is* everyone?"

"Mom's at work and Dad's cleaning out the gutters. Jake and Josh are holding the ladder, and Wally's picking up the stuff that comes out of the rainspouts," Peter told her.

"Yuck!" said Eddie. "Well, when they come in, would you give your brothers a message?"

"Okay," said Peter.

"Tell them that we're moving back to Ohio, and before we go, we want them to show us Smuggler's Cove, Knob Hill, and the old coal mine. Got it?"

There was silence at the other end of the line.

"Got it?" Eddie asked again.

"Does this mean you won't bake any more cookies for me?" came Peter's plaintive voice.

"I'm afraid so," Eddie said. "But we'll bake up a big batch just before we leave. Okay?"

"I'm going to be sad," said Peter.

"I know, buddy," said Eddie. "But that's life."

Two

Suspicion

Why, Wally wondered, when his mom worked in a hardware store, did the Hatfords have a rickety old ladder that had to be held on both sides when anyone climbed it? And why, when their dad was up on the ladder, did Jake and Josh get to hold it while he—Wally— had to scoop up the smelly muck that Mr. Hatford was hosing down the rainspouts?

Even though Wally was wearing his dad's work gloves, he hated the feel of soggy leaves, dead bugs, sharp twigs, and mold in his hands as he dumped it all into a trash barrel. When his father came down from the roof at last, Wally took off the gloves and threw them on the grass. Then he sprawled on the back steps beside the twins, who acted as though *they* had done all the work.

If I was the oldest boy in this family, there would be some changes around here, Wally thought. Jake and Josh shouldn't get the best jobs just because they were going into middle school in the fall. Peter, of course, being the youngest, didn't have to do half the work the others did, while Wally, in the middle, ten years old, got the short end of the stick. Again.

Peter appeared at the back screen.

"Eddie Malloy wants you to take her to Knob Hill and the old coal mine and Smuggler's Cove," he said.

Jake jerked upright. *"What?"*

"That's the message," said Peter.

"When? When does she want to go?"

"I dunno."

"Just Eddie?"

"All of them. Caroline and Beth, too, I guess."

"Why?" Jake asked.

Peter shrugged, lifting his small bony shoulders as high as they would go and then letting them drop.

"Did she call or come over?" asked Josh.

"She called."

"Peter, *think*!" Jake demanded. "Was that all she said?"

"Yes! I told you! They want to see Knob Hill and stuff before they go."

"Go *where?*" asked Wally.

"Back to Ohio," said Peter. "They're moving."

Like tires losing air, Wally and the twins sank slowly back into their sprawl on the steps. It was official, then. The Malloys were going home. After a year of Hatford tricks and teasing to drive them away, it had finally happened. The girls were going back.

"Well, hey! All *right*! It's about time!" said Jake, but no one else was cheering.

Peter came out on the steps and sat down beside his brothers. He and Wally looked somewhat alike. They had round faces and stocky builds, while the twins were string-bean skinny and already taller than their friends. "There won't be any more chocolate chunk peanut butter cookies," Peter said mournfully.

"Peter, don't you understand?" said Jake. "Once the Malloys are gone, the Bensons will be back! Our friends! They'll be living in their own house and it'll be just like old times! Nine guys together again! Laughs galore!"

"Hip hip hooray," Josh said without expression.

"I don't know what's wrong with the three of you," Jake said. "Don't tell me you're going soft. Don't tell me you're going to *miss* those girls!"

Wally wasn't sure he would *miss* them, exactly, but he'd certainly know they were gone. He'd used to think he would be supremely happy if he never saw Caroline Malloy and her sisters again. If he never had to feel Caroline poking him in the back with her ruler as she sat behind him at school. Never had to listen to Caroline bragging about how she had been moved up a grade—to *his* grade—because she was so "precocious" or watch Caroline stand up in front of the class to read a story and sound like she was an actress in Hollywood.

But now he wondered if, once she was gone, it would be like a big empty hole in the sky, like when the wind had blown down their locust tree and left only space where branches had been.

"So what are we going to do?" Wally asked Jake. "You know no one's supposed to go near that old mine. And she'll probably want to go up Knob Hill at night."

One of Jake's eyebrows tipped low toward his nose at one end and rose way up, like a question mark, at the other end. "You know what I think?" he said. "I think they're up to something. I'll bet Eddie's got some trick up her sleeve. I think she's trying to pull some big stunt on us before they go. And Smuggler's Cove? They've already been there! Done that! Oh, she's got it all figured out, you can bet."

No one spoke for a minute. Then Josh said, "Jake, you wouldn't trust the Malloys no matter what! How do you know that Eddie doesn't just want to be friends?"

Jake turned and stared at his twin, both of them dark with summer tans. "You think all Eddie Malloy wants is to be our *friend*?"

"Why not?" said Josh. "Maybe she's trying to get the most out of Buckman before they leave."

"Maybe the girls just want to show there are no hard feelings," said Wally.

"Yeah, and maybe the Pope's Protestant!" said Jake.

But even Peter chimed in. "Why do you always think the Malloys are bad?" he asked.

Jake rolled his eyes. "Okay, okay! Eddie's a kind and loyal friend. So we'll show them a good time! So we'll take them up Knob Hill and leave them there, for all I care! Tell her yes."

Wally looked around. "Who are you talking to?"

"Anyone! *I'm* not going to call her back. She didn't ask for me, did she, Peter?" said Jake.

Peter thought for a minute. "She asked if *anybody* was around."

"Okay. So, Wally, *you* call her," said Jake.

Wally had known that this would happen. No matter how much he wanted to stay clear of the Malloys, something always happened to rope him in. But not this time!

"Nope!" he said. "Not me. *I* never went around bragging about going in that coal mine or climbing up Knob Hill at night."

"Josh?" said Jake.

"Huh-uh," said Josh.

"Okay, Peter," said Jake. "Call Eddie back and tell her yes."

The boys went into the house and sat at the kitchen table while Peter dialed the Malloys' number. Wally sat with his chin in his hands. This was not going to end well, he was sure of it.

"Hello?" said Peter. "Eddie?" There was a pause. Then, "Jake said for me to call you. He said yes, he'll take you up Knob Hill and leave you there."

"Peter!" yelped Jake, springing from his chair. He grabbed the phone from his younger brother. "Joke! Joke!" he said to Eddie. "Sure, we'll show you around. Just let us know when you want to go."

■

Wally decided to mark off each day on his calendar until the Malloys were gone. Every day there wasn't a disaster was one less day to worry about.

But when Wally woke up the next morning and went downstairs, the Malloy girls were sitting on his front porch. Wally stared at them through the window, then turned and raced back upstairs and into the twins' bedroom.

"They're here!" he yelled.

Jake almost tumbled out of bed. "Huh?" he said. "Who?"

"The Malloys! They're sitting on our front porch with a picnic basket!"

"What?" yelled Josh, awake now.

All the commotion must have wakened Peter, because by the time Jake and Josh and Wally had pulled on their jeans and T-shirts and padded downstairs in their stocking feet, Peter was sitting out on the glider in his Donald Duck pajamas, the girls around him, laughing and talking.

"So where are we going today?" asked Beth pleasantly when she saw Peter's brothers. "Smuggler's Cove, Knob Hill, or the old coal mine?"

"Uh . . . ," Jake mumbled.

"We've brought a picnic basket," said Caroline. "Chicken salad sandwiches and grapes."

"And chocolate chunk cookies!" crowed Peter, wriggling his toes.

"Great!" said Jake, rubbing his eyes. "Let's make it Smuggler's Cove."

"Did you guys just get up?" asked Eddie.

"Of course not," said Jake. "You have to wait a minute, though, 'cause we've got to let Mom know where we're going." The rule was that they had to call their mother at the hardware store if they were going to be gone for more than an hour. Wally followed his brother inside.

"I don't like it!" Jake said. "This is a setup!"

Wally didn't know what to think. With Jake on the phone in the kitchen, though, and Josh and Peter out on the porch with the girls, he had a mad impulse to make a run for the stairs, dive into bed, and pull the covers over himself for the rest of the day. But maybe Mom would say they couldn't go and that would solve it. Maybe she'd say they hadn't finished their chores.

Jake came back from the kitchen.

"What'd she say?" asked Wally.

"To take Peter," said Jake morosely.

"Is that all?"

"Take Peter and have a good time."

And so, with a blanket tucked under his arm, Jake led the group down the porch steps. Wally carried a jug of water, and Josh took a bag of trail mix.

If they crossed the road in front of the house, they could go down the bank to the footbridge that led to Island Avenue and the house where the girls were staying. But this time they stayed on their side of the river and started down the road. After a mile or two, they would cut through a field and then the woods, and finally they would reach a rocky inlet circled by pine trees. Here the river lapped gently against the bank, and the crevasses between the rocks looked deep and forbidding. Smuggler's Cove was called that because according to legend, thieves used to smuggle knives and whiskey and furs down the river and hide them in the cove till they could find buyers in town. True or not, it was a good place to camp or have a picnic.

Well, okay, we're going on a picnic, Wally told himself. *That's all. Nothing to worry about.*

As they headed into the woods, Josh said, "Peter says you guys are really going to move back to Ohio. Is it for sure?"

"It's for sure," said Beth. "Dad's taken his old job back at the college, and he'll have our house ready for us when we get there. The Bensons will be here on the thirty-first. In fact, Mr. Benson's already back to start training the football team. He's staying at a hotel till the whole family arrives with their furniture."

Peter chugged along, still wearing his Donald Duck pj's, but he had put on his sneakers, too. "I'd rather have you than the Bensons," he said.

"Peter!" Jake exclaimed. "You're nuts!"

"Oh, you'll be glad to see them come back," Eddie told Peter. "You and the Benson guys have been friends for a long time. You won't even miss us once we're gone."

This was too easy, Wally thought. The Malloys were being too polite. There was probably poison on the grapes or something. And then he realized that he was sounding more and more like his brother Jake.

Three

■

Picnic, Sort Of

Whoever would have thought, Caroline wondered, that the Hatfords and the Malloys would be having a normal—no, even *pleasant*—picnic together without their parents? What she meant was that when parents were around, you more or less *had* to be polite, but here they were, not a mom or dad in sight, and they were acting like friends. They chose a mossy spot to spread the blanket.

"I thought maybe your dad was going to stick around and coach the high school football team," said Josh.

"He was thinking about it but decided to go back," said Beth.

"Are *you* sad?" Peter asked, his eyes on the cookie container.

"A little," said Beth.

"*I'm* going to miss the school," said Caroline.

All four Hatfords turned and stared at her.

"*School?*" said Wally.

"The auditorium. The stage," said Caroline. "We don't have a stage like that back home."

"Is that all you ever think about?" Josh asked her. "New York? Broadway?"

"Someday you'll see my name in lights," said Caroline. "You'll be visiting New York and you'll be walking along the street and you'll look up to see *Caroline Lenore Malloy* in lights. And you'll say to each other, 'She really meant it! She's an actress now!' "

"Oh, brother!" said Eddie.

"Well, we're going to have a great time when the Bensons come back," said Jake. "Man, we've known them our whole lives, practically. We're like brothers, almost."

"And *you're* like sisters!" said Peter, his face breaking into an angelic smile.

Jake groaned softly.

"You didn't treat us like sisters the last time we were here," said Eddie. "You tried to throw Caroline in the river."

"We treated you *exactly* as though you were sisters!" said Josh. "You followed us on a campout and tried to spy on us."

"Yeah," said Wally. "I woke up and found Caroline's hand creeping under the side of my tent. She was trying to throw my clothes in the river."

"Well, that's all water over the dam," said Eddie,

unwrapping the chicken salad. "We're only going to be here a few more weeks, so it would be nice if we all got along for a change."

Caroline stared at her sister. Had Eddie actually said *that*?

"This is all so polite, it's disgusting," said Jake. "We need some kind of excitement while we eat. Caroline, why don't you recite something creepy?"

Caroline did not think she had heard correctly. Someone was actually *asking* her to perform? One of the Hatfords? *Jake?* The truth was, Caroline was ready to perform at the drop of a hat. She had a very good memory for poems and stories.

"Um . . . I could do 'Little Orphant Annie,' " she said.

"Great," said Jake, passing around the grapes. "Let's hear it."

Caroline was not always sure she had every word in a poem correct when she recited it, but she figured that if the rhythm was right and the words made sense, it was good enough. She definitely remembered to say *orphant* instead of *orphan*.

"Should I stand up?" she asked.

"No, Caroline, just *do* it," said Eddie, rolling her eyes.

Caroline did, however, sit up on her knees to make herself a little taller. She swallowed and cleared her throat, waiting until the grapes had gone around the circle before she began in her most dramatic voice:

"Little Orphant Annie's come to our
 house to stay,
And wash the cups and saucers up, and
 brush the crumbs away,
And shoo the chickens off the porch,
 and dust the hearth, and sweep,
And make the fire, and bake the bread,
 and earn her board-and-keep . . ."

"Her what?" asked Peter.
"Her allowance," said Wally. "Shhh."
Caroline continued:

"And all us other children, when the
 supper-things is done,
We set around the kitchen fire and has
 the mostest fun
A-listenin' to the witch-tales that Annie
 tells about,
And the Goblins that'll git you
If you don't watch out!"

Peter's eyes were wide open at this point. Jake and
Josh were smirking, as usual, but people always en-
joyed this poem when Caroline recited it, especially
the goblin part. She went on:

"Once there was a little boy who wouldn't
 say his prayers,
And when he went to bed at night,
 away upstairs . . ."

20

At that moment Caroline felt a tickle down her spine and was thrilled to think she could recite something so expressively that it affected even *her*!

> *"His Mammy heard him holler, and his*
> *Daddy heard him bawl . . ."*

A creeping, crawling sensation replaced the tickle. She gave a little shudder.

> *"And when they turned the covers down,*
> *he wasn't there at all!"*

Now the crawling sensation was moving sideways, not up and down. Suddenly Caroline began grabbing frantically at her back and sides. "There's a bug on me!" she shrieked. "There's a bug down my shirt!"

"And I think I know who put it there," said Eddie, glancing at Jake, who had moved just a little too close to Caroline and was scooting away as fast as he could.

"Get it out!" Caroline screamed, scrambling to her feet and jumping up and down. She had never been fond of bugs, but she had also never had one dropped down her shirt before, and now she was half crazy. "Get it out!" she kept screaming. "Aaaah! Help! Eddie! Oh, it's crawling all over me!"

Jake rolled on the ground laughing as Caroline jiggled and danced and swatted and clawed, until finally a black beetle dropped onto the blanket from beneath her T-shirt.

"Man, I wish I had a camera!" said Josh, holding his

sides. "Caroline, you could go onstage for comedy night with that act!"

Even Peter was laughing, but Caroline was still screaming.

"You can stop now, Caroline!" Jake hooted. "It's dead, after all your bashing."

"Okay, that's enough entertainment," said Eddie. "Let's eat. I'll make the sandwiches. Chicken salad for everybody." She opened the loaf of bread and began, passing along a sandwich for each of them.

Caroline was mortified and angry. It was rude to interrupt an actress like that. If that had happened in a theater in New York, the stage manager would have rushed out from behind the curtain to help; the ushers would have taken the person who had done it straight up the aisle and out the door.

"Okay, go ahead, Caroline. No more bugs," Jake promised.

But Caroline said, "I think you were mean and rotten to do that, and if you want to know what happens next in the poem, you'll have to read it yourself."

"No, thanks," said Jake.

"Well, *I* want to hear the rest!" said Peter.

"Tell that to your brothers," Caroline muttered. Was nobody going to come to her aid? Eddie and Beth just went on passing around food; Jake and Josh and Wally took turns digging their hands into the sack of chips. Nobody besides Peter really wanted to hear the rest of the poem, and she hadn't even got to the part about the girl who was snatched through the ceiling!

Caroline kept her head down as she nibbled around the crust of her sandwich and tried to pretend she had forgotten the incident. But actresses never forgot. Now she knew how it felt when a play bombed and there was no encore. How it felt when people left at intermission. Sometimes, she knew, audiences even hooted and booed.

That's okay, Caroline told herself. She would learn how to take humiliation. She would learn to accept defeat. She would use this sad performance as a stepping-stone of courage and perseverance, and even if there was only one member of the audience left in a theater, Caroline would perform for that person alone, for always . . . *always* . . . the show must go on.

"Hey!" came Jake's voice.

Caroline looked up. Jake had his chicken sandwich in one hand and was fishing around inside his mouth with the other.

"What *is* this?" he said, spitting something out.

It was small. It was black. It was mangled. But Caroline could make out what it was—or what it had been: the black beetle that had been dropped down her shirt.

"We're just returning the favor, Jake!" Eddie laughed. "Give your sandwich a little spice."

"Yuck!" said Jake, spitting out even more.

"It's dead, after all," Eddie taunted. "You're not afraid of a dead bug, are you?"

"Three more weeks and you'll be back in Ohio," said Jake. "Then you can torment somebody back there. I'll bet your neighbors can't wait."

"You started it," said Eddie. "We invited you to a picnic, and look what happened."

"Okay, we're sorry," said Josh. "Where did you want to go next?"

"How about Knob Hill?" said Eddie. "In the dark. About midnight, maybe?"

■　■　■　■　■　■　■　■　■　■

Four

■

Mystery

It seemed to Wally as though Jake and Eddie just couldn't help themselves. They were going to go on fighting and teasing forever. No matter how much fun the Hatfords and the Malloys might be having together, no matter how little time there was left, Jake and Eddie had to go on competing, tricking, scheming, until it would be almost impossible to stay friends.

Polite as they all had been—up to the bug episode, anyway—Jake and Eddie had argued about the best place to lay the blanket. Eddie had said they were too close to the river, and Jake had said they weren't close enough. They'd argued about who had eaten most of the grapes and who had pitched the most home runs on their ball team.

"You know what we ought to do? We ought to take

them to the top of Knob Hill and leave them!" said Josh, putting Wally's feelings into words.

Going to Knob Hill and the old Indian burial ground was delayed, however, because both the girls and the boys knew that their parents would never allow them to go out at midnight, not even if they left Peter behind. In fact, they wouldn't even be allowed to go that far after dark. The neighborhood, yes. The business district, yes. But not out to the country, where there weren't even streetlights to help them see where they were going.

Besides, Mrs. Hatford had given the boys a job before she'd gone to work that morning.

"Mrs. Malloy needs all the boxes she can get for packing," she had told them. "I think it would be a very neighborly thing for you to go around to some of the stores downtown and see if they have any empties. I can get big boxes from the hardware store, but I'm sure the Malloys could use some smaller sizes too."

It wasn't a job that appealed to Wally, but their mother had a way of making them feel guilty about saying no. Besides, the guy at the drugstore sometimes gave them jelly beans. So Wally went into the living room, where Peter was putting a puzzle together on the coffee table.

"You wanna go look for empty boxes?" Wally asked.

"What do I get if I do?" asked Peter.

"Jelly beans, maybe," said Wally.

"What do I get if I don't?"

"A kick in the pants," Wally joked.

"Oh, all right," said Peter. "But it's hot out there!"

"Well, Jake's going to his baseball game and Josh is going to the library to help paint a mural. I can't go anywhere if you don't come too," said Wally, knowing that the boys were never, under any circumstances, to leave Peter at home by himself. Mrs. Hatford clerked six days a week at the hardware store, and Mr. Hatford delivered the mail, so if neither of Wally's brothers was going to be around, that left him in charge.

They went down the sidewalk, toward the business district, Peter lagging a foot or two behind Wally.

"The sidewalk feels hot even with sneakers on," Peter complained.

"Try walking one inch above the sidewalk," Wally teased.

"Huh?" said Peter.

"Or you could spit on your feet. That'll keep 'em cool," Wally added, grinning. And then, when Peter got ready to try it, he said, "Hey, Peter. No!"

They stopped at Oldakers' Bookstore first, and it was like heaven to step inside the air-conditioned room.

"How you doin'?" called Mike, the owner.

"Any empty boxes?" Wally asked. "We're collecting them for the Malloys. They're going back to Ohio."

"So I heard," said Mike. "I got some early calendars in this morning. You'll find the boxes in the back."

"Thanks," said Wally. He and Peter walked down the rows of mysteries and science fiction novels and through the café at the back, until they came to the

27

stockroom. Three empty boxes sat just inside the door. Wally picked up two, Peter got the other, and they carried them back outside.

At the drugstore, Mr. Larkin told them they could have the boxes that some chocolate syrup had come in. He winked at Wally. "And how would you guys like a handful of jelly beans?"

"I wouldn't mind!" said Peter.

Wally was never sure about those jelly beans, though, because Mr. Larkin never took them out of the jelly bean jar. He would open a drawer beside the cash register and take the jelly beans from there. Were those the ones that had fallen on the floor, maybe?

"Thanks," Wally said as the druggist dumped a fistful into the two outstretched hands.

A yellow jelly bean in Wally's hand had dark marks on one side. Had somebody kicked it with a shoe? he wondered. A red jelly bean looked faded. Had someone sucked on it for a second or two and then spit it out? Peter put all his jelly beans in his mouth at once, but Wally ate them one by one, exploring them a bit with his tongue.

With two more boxes added to their load, Wally gave Peter the smallest, and he carried the rest. Ethel's Bakery was next.

"I flattened all my boxes yesterday," Ethel told them, "but I can give you one that my flour came in this morning."

Peter put it on his head upside down. There was just enough flour in it to give his hair a fine white coating, so that he looked like a little old man.

"We've got enough," Wally told him. "We'll tell Jake and Josh to get the rest. Let's go home."

■

"It's certainly going to be different around here with the Malloys gone," said Mrs. Hatford that evening at dinner.

"Maybe," said her husband. "But with the Bensons coming back, things won't be any quieter, that's for sure. Five boys in place of three girls can never be quieter."

"I just wish I'd been a better neighbor," said Wally's mother. "It couldn't have been easy for Jean to move down here with her family for a year, not knowing a living soul, and having to fit in with the faculty wives and do all that university stuff. We should have had them for dinner more often."

"We had them for Thanksgiving, remember?" said Mr. Hatford. "Besides, you work full-time, Ellen. Jean Malloy didn't expect you to do more."

"It just would have been nice if I could have been more helpful," said Mrs. Hatford. "I think I'll have them over for brunch right after the van leaves on moving day. I'll tell them to stop by here for a bite before they go. They'll surely appreciate that."

"I know they will," said her husband.

■

Jake managed to find a couple of boxes at a filling station, and Josh got one from next door.

"After dinner," Mrs. Hatford said, "you boys take these boxes on over to Mrs. Malloy and ask if there's anything else we can do. I'll call her myself and invite her for brunch on moving day."

All the boxes had been piled on the front porch, and after dinner the four boys set to work separating them into four piles, one for each of them to carry. Some had grit at the bottom and had to be turned over and tapped. Some had bunches of rolled-up paper, or store receipts.

Wally was stacking the pile of boxes he would carry and shook out some dust. A small piece of paper fluttered out too. It was just a shopping list, and he had started to throw it out when something caught his eye. He read it again: *Eggs, Rope, Tomato sauce, Flashlight, Dynamite.*

"Hey!" he said.

Jake looked up. "What?"

"Dynamite!" said Wally.

"Huh?" Jake reached over and took the slip of paper from him. "Dynamite?" he said. "Where would you go to buy dynamite?"

"Where you'd go to buy rope and a flashlight, I guess," said Wally. "Doesn't that sound sort of suspicious to you? Rope, flashlight, dynamite?"

The boys stared at the paper some more.

"I don't know. Eggs and tomato sauce don't sound too dangerous to me," said Josh.

"Maybe this isn't a list of stuff to get from one store. Maybe it's a list of things from several stores," said Jake.

The boys looked at each other. What *did* someone

want with rope and a flashlight and dynamite? Wally took the note back and stuffed it in his pocket. He wasn't letting go of *this*!

■

Wally didn't sleep very well that night. Maybe he should walk that piece of paper down to the police station and turn it over to the sergeant on duty, he thought. No, it was too ridiculous.

But as the night went on, Wally worried. What if he *didn't* turn that paper over to the police and then there was a big explosion? What if *then* he rushed it down to the police station and the officer said, "Why, anybody knows this is the handwriting of Mad Bomber Bill, Wally. If we had seen this list in time, we could have checked his house over, looked in his garage to see if he had any explosives."

And maybe Mad Bomber Bill had a little nephew who always followed him around. And on that particular day Mad Bomber Bill told the little boy to stay home.

"Go on back to your mother and quit following me around," Mad Bomber Bill might have said.

But maybe the little boy was too fond of his uncle and only pretended he was going home. Maybe he turned around and kept following his uncle, hiding behind trees all the way. And maybe Mad Bomber Bill went into somebody's house to place the dynamite. And when he came back out to light the fuse, the little boy ran inside to see what his uncle had put in there that was so secret.

And then maybe the fuse started to burn, and as it got closer and closer to the dynamite, Mad Bomber Bill saw his little nephew playing around inside the house, and maybe he called, "No! Come out! Come out!" But maybe it was too late and the little boy stumbled and the dynamite went off and . . .

"No!" yelled Wally.

His eyes popped open. There was complete silence in the house. His room was dark.

Suddenly he heard a door open at the end of the hall, and a few moments later his mom came in.

"Wally?" she said. "Was that you?"

"Was who me?" said Wally, his heart pounding.

"I just heard someone yell, and it sounded like you," said his mother.

Wally's head whirled and he tried to think. "It was Bill," he said.

"Who?" said his mother.

"A dream," said Wally.

"Are you okay?" she asked.

"Maybe," said Wally.

"Then go back to sleep," she told him.

"Okay," said Wally. But he heard the grandfather clock in the hall downstairs chime out one, then two, then three o'clock before he finally fell asleep.

■ ■ ■ ■ ■ ■ ■ ■ ■ ■ ■

Five

■

Dare

"I don't know why you told the Hatfords that we'll go to Knob Hill some night at midnight," Beth said to Eddie. "You know Mom will never let us."

"Yeah, but the Hatfords won't be able to go either, so it will make it sound as though *they're* the ones who chicken out," said Eddie. "I just like to keep them on the hot seat. Didn't you see how suspicious they were acting at Smuggler's Cove, like I was going to pull something on them? It drives them nuts when we're polite. Now we can sit back and see what they come up with."

"It looks like they're going on a safari," Caroline said, glancing out the kitchen window. Beth and Eddie turned to look, and coming up the hill from the river were the four Hatford boys, each carrying a load of boxes on his head, each load balanced by a pair of hands.

Mrs. Malloy came into the room just then. "What in the world . . . ?" she said, going to the back door.

"Empty boxes from Mom," said Wally as they stepped up onto the porch. "She thought maybe you could use them for packing."

"How thoughtful of her!" said Mrs. Malloy. "Of course we can use them! Moving always takes more boxes than you think. Just stack them there in the front hallway, would you, boys?"

The Hatfords walked through the kitchen and the dining room and deposited their load in the front hallway while the girls watched.

"Do you have time to stay for some cookies and iced tea?" said Mrs. Malloy.

Was that a serious question? Caroline wondered. Did boys have stomachs?

"Yes!" said Peter, answering for them, and they all went back to the kitchen and sat around the big table, where the girls were just finishing their dinner. Mrs. Malloy put a platter of brownies and sugar cookies on the table, along with a pitcher and some paper cups. Then she left the kitchen to carry a few of the boxes upstairs.

Jake looked slyly around the table. "Question," he said. "If somebody told you he was going to buy some rope, a flashlight, and some dynamite, what would you think he was going to do?"

"Hmm," said Eddie. "If he needed a flashlight, then he was probably going to be working at night."

"If he had rope, then he was probably going to lower

himself down a cliff or into a hole or something," said Beth.

"Or hide the dynamite somewhere," said Caroline.

"What is this? A game?" asked Eddie.

"I don't know," said Jake. "Show her the list, Wally."

Wally pulled the small slip of paper from his pocket and handed it to Eddie.

" 'Eggs, Rope, Tomato sauce, Flashlight, Dynamite,' " she read aloud. She studied it for a moment. "Nothing in code? No map? No 'X marks the spot'?"

"I didn't say it meant anything," Jake said quickly. "It just seems sort of unusual, that's all. Wally found it in one of the empty boxes."

Wally took the paper back and put it in his pocket again.

"Of course," said Eddie, "if they *were* connected somehow—the rope, the flashlight, and the dynamite—we're probably the first ones to find out. So if anything happens . . ."

"We're just going to sit around and wait until it happens?" asked Josh.

"So what do you suggest?" said Beth. "Taking it to the police and telling them we've found a suspicious shopping list?"

"Just keeping our eyes open, that's all," said Jake.

"If somebody *was* going to blow up something, and somebody *was* going to lower himself down into a hole somewhere, where would that somewhere be?" said Eddie.

"It could be anywhere at all," said Josh, reaching for

a cookie. "Somebody's basement. The riverbank. The old coal mine."

Caroline's mind was already alive with possibilities. What an exciting movie that would make! A story! A play! What if *she* were being lowered on a rope into a gravel pit? A mine? What if *she* had to blow up a dam to prevent the enemy from taking over a town?

Maybe her job would be to *stop* an explosion, to reach the fuse in time. The clock would be ticking, and Caroline would be lowered into the hole to stomp on the lit fuse before the bomb went off. Her eyes glazed over. Her pulse began to race. *Seventeen, sixteen, fifteen, fourteen . . . ,* she counted down to herself.

Eddie snapped her fingers in front of Caroline's face. "Hey!" she said. "Get a grip."

Caroline blinked. "It *could* be serious," she said.

"Yeah, well, if we hear of anything suspicious, we'll let you know," said Jake.

"About that old coal mine . . . ," said Eddie, and Caroline could tell that Jake was uncomfortable. "You and the Benson guys used to go in there, right?"

"Well, not exactly, because it's been fenced in," said Jake. "There's just the tunnel into the mountain."

Eddie's eyes narrowed. "So you've only been over the fence?"

"Um . . . not exactly," said Jake.

"You guys haven't even been *near* that old coal mine!" Eddie scoffed. "It's all hot air! It's all talk!"

"We have so been near it!" said Jake. "I've looked in there a thousand times!"

"Well, *I'm* going to go *in* it!" said Eddie. "I'm not

going to leave Buckman until I've seen inside that old coal mine."

Caroline and Beth looked at their sister in horror. Every so often Eddie did that. She just went out on a limb and said she was going to do things she never could. Or never should.

"Is there barbed wire on the top of the fence?" Eddie asked.

"No," said Josh, "but it's a tall fence. Ten feet tall."

"Is there a guard on duty?"

"No, but the sheriff drives by once in a while."

"Is there a guard dog inside the fence?"

"Not that I've seen," said Jake, "but—"

"Then I'm going in," said Eddie.

"When?" asked Wally, looking astonished.

"I don't know. I'll have to case the place first. Anybody going in with me?"

"Not me," said Beth. "You're nuts, Eddie."

"Not me," said Caroline.

Eddie looked at the Hatfords.

"I'm not going in any coal mine!" said Peter. "You're really going to get in trouble, Eddie. My dad said never, ever, *ever* go there!"

"I'm not going either," said Wally.

"Count me out," said Josh.

Eddie looked at Jake. There was a long pause.

"Okay," Jake said. "If you find a way, I'm in."

Caroline and Beth exchanged glances. They were not going to move out of Buckman. They were going to be *kicked* out of Buckman, Caroline was sure.

■ ■ ■ ■ ■ ■ ■ ■ ■ ■ ■

Six

■

Shadows

"**W**hy didn't you tell her no?" Wally asked Jake as they went back across the swinging bridge in the near-darkness. "You'll only get in trouble, and you know it!"

"And have her call me chicken?" said Jake. "Relax. There's no way she can get in. The joke's on her. I'll go along like I'm ready to go in, and it'll be up to her to find a way to open the gate, which she won't be able to do."

"I don't like it," said Josh. "Eddie's going to keep pushing the limits until she makes us do something we don't want to."

"Who says I don't want to?" Jake asked. "If she finds a way to get in, I'll go too."

Wally didn't like this. Why couldn't the Malloys go? Just *go! Now!* Before anything happened.

"Don't say anything to Mom," Jake warned Peter as they approached their house.

"I *won't*! What do you think I am? A tattletale?" Peter asked.

As Wally lay in bed that night, he decided he was in the clear. Their parents would not let them go out at midnight, so he could stop worrying about the old Indian burial ground. He had told Jake and Eddie he would not go with them inside the old coal mine, so he wouldn't get in trouble there. They had already been to Smuggler's Cove, and nothing much had happened, so he was home free. Let Jake get in trouble. He was just asking for it.

Wally began to relax. He didn't have to show up at the Malloys' ever again if he didn't want to. He could spend the rest of the summer doing exactly what he wanted, which was . . . well, nothing.

Not exactly nothing, though. Because what was nothing to someone else might be something to Wally. For example, he was looking forward to spending one whole day trying to figure out how many different calls a mockingbird could make. He wanted to sit out on the porch and listen when a mockingbird perched on top of a telephone pole and began to sing. Usually the bird repeated each song twice, which would give Wally a chance to write down the call: *robin, cardinal, wren, blue jay* . . . But of course he didn't recognize all birdcalls, so maybe he should take a recorder. . . .

Or maybe he would like to go a whole morning with his hand over his right eye, and all afternoon with his hand over his left, just to see which eye was stronger.

Or maybe he would climb through the trapdoor in

the attic leading to the widow's walk on the roof, and sit up there on that little balcony and see if he could tell whenever the wind changed direction.

There was no end to the things Wally Hatford could think of to do on his own. Sometimes he just liked to get on his bike and ride around town. He'd try to memorize the streets going east from the library, and then the streets going west. Or he'd go to the Dairy Store and ask for a cup of "Today's Flavor" without knowing what it was, and then he would taste it and see if he could guess. Some people might think that Wally's life was boring, he knew, but there were so many things going on in his head, he didn't have a chance to be bored.

It was hot outside, though, even at night. Peter was right; during the day you couldn't step on the sidewalk barefoot. It was one of the hottest summers the East had ever had, the newspaper said—over a hundred degrees for five days in a row, even here in West Virginia. Maybe what Wally *ought* to do was wait until about two o'clock in the afternoon someday and then see if he really could fry an egg on the sidewalk.

Finally, hot and sweaty, Wally fell asleep, and he woke up even warmer than he'd been when he'd gone to bed. He rolled over and sat up, waiting to see if he could smell pancakes or anything. He couldn't. That meant it wasn't Sunday. He'd almost lost track of the days of the week.

He listened for any clink or clunk of spoons and bowls in the kitchen to tell him whether the twins were awake. He didn't hear any. But he did think he heard voices coming from somewhere, so he pulled on his shorts and T-shirt and went downstairs.

Not again! There were the Malloy girls sitting out on his front porch, and there was Peter with a fistful of chocolate chip cookies.

Wally's first thought was to ignore them and go to the kitchen for cereal. But he went upstairs instead and stuck his head into the twins' bedroom. "They're here again," he said.

For a moment nothing happened. Then Jake rolled over and opened one eye. "What are you talking about?" he asked crossly.

"I just thought you'd want to know: the Malloys are sitting out on the front porch, feeding Peter chocolate chip cookies," Wally said. Then he went back downstairs, through the hall, and into the kitchen, poured himself some Cap'n Crunch cereal, and mixed it with Cocoa Puffs.

Down the stairs came Jake and Josh. Wally could hear them whispering together in the hall. They crept into the kitchen.

"I'm not going out there," said Josh.

"Me neither," said Jake. "Peter can sit out there in his Donald Duck pajamas all day if he wants. But we didn't invite the girls over." He took a bowl out of the cupboard, filled it to the top with Cocoa Puffs, and got the milk from the fridge.

The twins had just sat down at the table when they heard the front door open and Peter say, "Come on out to the kitchen. You want some cereal?"

Jake was still in his boxer shorts and Josh was in his

pajama bottoms. Upsetting the milk carton, Jake leaped from his chair and flew out the back door, Josh behind him. When the Malloy girls got to the kitchen, there was nothing to see but Wally calmly eating his Cocoa Puffs, and milk dripping onto the floor.

"Well!" said Eddie. "What have we here?"

"I invited them in for breakfast," Peter told Wally, smiling broadly.

"It's okay, Peter. We've already had breakfast," said Beth. "Where are Jake and Josh?"

There was the soft sound of the front door opening, then of footsteps on the hall stairs.

"They'll be down in a minute," Wally said, and went on reading the comics.

Beth got a sponge from the sink and cleaned up the milk on the table and the floor. Then the girls sat down—like they owned the place, Wally thought.

When Jake and Josh entered the kitchen, dressed, they tried to act as though they'd just got up. It was too ridiculous.

"We've decided we want to see Knob Hill even if we have to go in daylight," Eddie said. "So, we're ready."

"Sure, why not?" Jake said, and poured himself another bowl of cereal.

"I found something really interesting," said Beth. "I went to the Internet to look up Knob Hill and found out all sorts of fascinating things about it. Want to hear?"

"Sure," said Josh. He put the milk back in the fridge.

" 'Knob Hill, Buckman, West Virginia,' " Beth read

from a piece of paper she'd pulled out of her pocket. " 'This rounded hill west of the city was once the burial ground for a little-known tribe of Native Americans, known as the Shanatee. They were both admired and feared by neighboring tribes, due to a superstition regarding their shadows. It was said that if, on Knob Hill, the shadow of any person were to fall on the shadow of another, they would be the next two persons to die. When the tribes fought, therefore, neighboring warriors were reluctant go up the hill, for fear their shadows would touch. For this reason, the Shanatee had full possession of Knob Hill for many years, until the tribe mysteriously disappeared. It is generally believed that an epidemic wiped out this short-lived tribe, but legend has it that when the chief warrior died, the tribe committed mass suicide by walking across the face of the land and allowing their shadows to commingle.' "

Beth stopped and looked around. "Well! What do you think of that?"

The Hatford boys sat speechless. They had never bothered to look up Knob Hill on the Internet. They hadn't known about the shadows.

"So," said Eddie. "I want to go see this place."

Wally glanced at his brothers. It was another hot day—too hot, really, to go climbing. But that wasn't what he was worried about. As long as the sun was shining, one of their shadows was bound to fall on someone else's.

■

Fifteen minutes later, they were all walking across a pasture toward the high round hill, Peter taking big steps to keep up, the stubble of grass and weeds pricking his short legs. Everyone seemed to be spreading out as they started up the hill, keeping their shadows definitely separate from each other.

It took longer than they'd thought it would to get to the top. They grew hotter with every step, but at last, when they reached the crest, there was a bit more breeze, which helped dry the perspiration that dripped down their faces.

"So this is it, huh?" Eddie said, her voice hushed and reverent. "Where the Shanatee are buried? Doesn't it sort of spook you out that we might be standing on the very grave of one of their warriors?" She moved a step closer to Jake, and instantly Jake took a step closer to Josh. Their shadows almost touched, and Josh jumped.

They fanned out some more, studying the ground, stepping on large rocks strewn here and there. Suddenly Jake knelt down and said, "Hey! Look what I found!"

Caroline hurried over, getting just close enough to see him holding an almost perfect arrowhead. "It was just lying there? You found it just like that?" she asked.

"I kicked it," said Jake. "There are supposed to be a lot up here."

Instantly the girls began kicking at the ground with the toes of their sneakers. Beth even got down on her knees and began digging around the rocks. Eddie seemed especially intent on finding another arrowhead.

Jake and Josh and Wally and Peter worked to stay off each other's shadows. The girls didn't seem that concerned, Wally thought, but he didn't believe in taking chances.

At last Eddie said, "Hey, Jake, can I see that arrowhead a second? I want to know what to look for."

"Sure," Jake said.

Eddie turned it over and over in her hand. "You're a big fat liar, Jake," she said.

"What d'you mean?" asked Jake. "That's a real Indian arrowhead, and I can prove it."

"Yeah, but you didn't just find it this morning," said Eddie. "It doesn't have a speck of dirt on it. Not even dust! It even looks like it's been polished! You brought this along this morning, just as a joke."

Jake laughed. "Well, it worked, didn't it? You and Beth down on your hands and knees, digging away . . ." He and Josh hooted.

But Wally was sitting on a rock, reading the folded-up paper that Beth had read to them that morning. Somehow she had dropped it while she was searching for arrowheads.

"You know what else is fake?" he said. "The Shanatee Indians."

Beth jumped up and tried to grab the paper, but Wally held it away from her.

"It is not fake!" said Beth. "I printed it right off the encyclopedia on the computer."

"Some encyclopedia!" said Wally. "It misspelled *possession* and *epidemic*."

Beth's face began to color. Everyone knew that the

one thing Wally Hatford could do well was spell. "And the Shanatee Indians, if there *were* Indians," Wally continued, "wouldn't have called it Knob Hill. What kind of an Indian name is that?"

There was nothing for Beth and Eddie and Caroline to do but laugh.

"So, okay, we're even. You fell for it, didn't you—the shadows and everything? We had you scared half out of your shorts," Eddie said.

"That's part of the story Beth submitted to the short story contest at the library," Caroline told the boys. "She's good, isn't she? If she wins, she'll get it published in the newspaper."

"So you just made the whole thing up?" Wally asked.

"Totally," said Beth.

"There weren't any Shanatee Indians?" asked Peter.

"Nope."

"And all that stuff about shadows is nonsense?" asked Josh.

"Completely," said Eddie. "We had you guys hornswoggled, but good!"

■ ■ ■ ■ ■ ■ ■ ■ ■ ■ ■

Seven

■

Center Stage

For many days, the Hatfords and the Malloys didn't see much of each other. It was almost too hot to go outside. Eddie's baseball games, which were keeping the girls there till the end of summer, almost fizzled because the players were so exhausted by the heat.

People stayed in their air-conditioned houses or went to the movies or the pool. Beth spent her days at the library, working on her short fantasy story about the make-believe Shanatee Indians and helping to shelve books in her spare time. Whenever the girls were home, there was packing to do, and slowly the drawers and closets were emptying as more and more boxes piled up in the living room, ready for the movers. It was depressing, Caroline thought.

Twice she had crept into the elementary school when only the custodian was around and had gone into the empty auditorium and up onstage, where she recited, very softly but with the most dramatic gestures she could think of, the scene for a play or a story of her own.

What she had to do before she left Buckman, she told herself, was recite the poem "The Raven" from the stage. The whole thing. A few weeks earlier, she had done an Internet search for her name, Caroline Lenore Malloy, wondering if anyone, anywhere, might know of her—if a newspaper might have picked up the story of her being carried down the Buckman River, for example, the day she fell in. With trembling fingers she had typed her name, and she had got thirty-four pages of references. The only problem was that none of them said *Caroline Lenore Malloy.* They only said *Caroline* or *Lenore* or *Malloy.* But one of those hits was "The Raven," a poem by Edgar Allan Poe with the name *Lenore* in it: "*. . . sorrow for the lost Lenore.*"

Lenore was not a common name. In fact, Caroline had never heard of a single other person with that name. It was this that made her decide she simply had to memorize that poem, and once she had memorized it, she had to recite it somewhere onstage.

When she found the poem at the library, however, she was discouraged by how long it was. So far she had only memorized the first two stanzas, but she was working on it.

She had to be careful when she slipped into the school. It wasn't allowed, for one thing. None of the students were allowed inside the building until

September. Once in a while, she knew, the principal came by, but usually only the custodian was there working—tightening door handles, painting a wall, repairing a desk, changing lightbulbs, getting the old school ready for another year of classes in the fall. Classes without Caroline.

Caroline would sit in a swing or climb on the monkey bars on the playground until she was sure the custodian was working in another part of the building, far from the auditorium. Then she would slip through the unlocked side door, creep down the hall to the auditorium, and enter the cool darkness of that wonderful room.

Now, on this particular morning so close to moving day, Caroline knew she was going onstage in Buckman for the very last time. She walked down the long sloping aisle to the foot of the stage and climbed the four steps at one side that led behind the curtain.

She stood looking upward, entranced by the various ropes and pulleys. Everything looked very old and very used, and she could hardly bear the thought that the next time the big velvet curtain was opened and closed, or the backdrop of a meadow was lowered, she would not be here with the spotlight shining on her.

No matter. This was Caroline's day, and slowly, with style and grace, she moved to center stage. In a soft voice, she addressed the empty seats in front of her:

"I would like to recite a little bit of 'The Raven,' by Edgar Allan Poe," she said, clasping her hands in front of her, her voice taking on a note of mystery and terror.

> "Once upon a midnight dreary,
>   while I pondered, weak and weary,
> Over many a quaint and curious volume
>   of forgotten lore . . ."

Caroline was good at memorizing. She was precocious, of course, so she could remember a lot, but things like the multiplication table were lowest on her priority list, while poetry (especially dramatic, sad, and tragic poetry—in particular, poems with her name in them) was number one.

> "While I nodded, nearly napping,
>   suddenly there came a tapping,
> As of someone gently rapping, rapping
>   at my chamber door.
> ' 'Tis some visitor,' I muttered, 'tapping
>   at my chamber door—
> Only this and nothing more.' "

As Caroline went on, her words echoed in the empty auditorium, and—inspired by her own inflections—she let her voice soar:

> "Ah, distinctly I remember it was in
>   the bleak December,
> And each separate dying ember wrought
>   its ghost upon the floor."

And now came the part with *her* name in it—the name of the beautiful girl, Lenore, whom Poe was writing about, who had died young and would be in his heart forever. At that moment, however, Caroline saw the custodian start to pass the auditorium door, then stop.

She had an audience! Someone was listening to her! Caroline knew that at any moment he would ask what she was doing here, how she had got into the school, and he would demand that she leave at once. So she had to make good use of the time. At her middle name, Lenore, she decided, she would fall into a dead faint there onstage. She would expire right in front of her audience—an audience of one—and would pull the curtain closed at the same time. A finer, more dramatic finish she could not imagine.

> *"Eagerly I wished the morrow;*
> *vainly I had sought to borrow*
> *From my books surcease of sorrow*
> *—sorrow for the lost Lenore . . ."*

Caroline's eyes began to close as her hand grabbed for the rope to pull the curtain.

> *"For . . . the rare . . . and radiant maiden . . .*
> *whom the angels name . . . Lenore . . ."*

She touched the rope, then grasped it with both hands and pulled with all her strength as she let her knees collapse. . . .

"Nameless here for evermore!"

Wham!

The curtain didn't budge, but the large painted canvas backdrop of a meadow came crashing down on Caroline. She was pinned to the floor with her legs and one arm caught beneath the backdrop. *Ouch!*

She could hear running footsteps coming down the aisle.

"Hey!" the custodian was calling. "Hey! Are you all right?"

Caroline closed her eyes.

The footsteps were coming up the side steps now. Then they were crossing the stage.

"What the heck?" the custodian was saying. "What are you doing in here?"

Caroline's lips moved. *"Darkness there and nothing more,"* she whispered.

"What?" said the custodian, quickly pulling on the rope that lifted the canvas.

" *'Tis the wind and nothing more,"* said Caroline.

"Didn't you go to school here last year?" the custodian asked, studying her closely as the scenery rose in the air.

And Caroline answered, *"Quoth the Raven, 'Nevermore.' "*

■ ■ ■ ■ ■ ■ ■ ■ ■ ■ ■

Eight

■

Emergency

Wally was sitting on the roof of his house when he heard the siren. Josh had taken Peter to Jake and Eddie's summer baseball game, but Wally said that if he was going to be roasted alive, he'd do it where there was a little breeze, thank you.

Besides, shade from the beech tree fell on the widow's walk—the small fenced-in patch of roof with the trapdoor in the middle that led down to the attic. It was supposedly the place where the wives of sea captains stood, looking out to the ocean for any sight of their long-lost husbands. Except that there was no ocean in Buckman. Only the river, not more than three feet deep in most places.

Wally had been standing perfectly still, trying to see if he could detect the direction of the wind. Actually, it was so hot and still and humid that he couldn't feel any wind at all. *It must be a hundred and ten degrees up here,* he thought, and he wondered if he could fry an egg on the shingles.

Then he heard the ambulance coming down College Avenue, and he saw it turning in, farther on, at the school.

What could have happened at the school? Wally asked himself. Nobody was there! It was vacation. Maybe the custodian had fallen off a ladder or something. Wally quickly crawled through the trapdoor and climbed down the ladder to the attic floor, then the stairs to the second floor, then the stairs all the way down to the first.

He jumped onto his bike and was halfway up the street toward the school when he saw the ambulance pulling out of the school driveway and heading for the hospital.

Wally pedaled as fast as he could, forgetting the heat. At last he would have something exciting to tell the family at dinner. Nobody else seemed interested in Wally's observations on mockingbirds or wind direction, but he knew he could capture the twins' attention, at least, if he could say he had chased an ambulance all the way to the hospital.

It wasn't far, and when Wally got there, he could see the two attendants wheeling somebody in on a stretcher.

Wally left his bike by the door and ran inside. The attendants were heading toward a glass door farther on. Wally raced after them and found Caroline

Malloy on the stretcher with her hands crossed over her chest.

"Caroline!" Wally gasped.

"Wally!" she said weakly, sounding as though she might cry.

But before they could say any more, the glass door closed in his face. All he could think was that maybe there had been an explosion at the school and that Mad Bomber Bill had got Caroline and it was all Wally's fault for not showing that shopping list with *Dynamite* on it to the police.

Wally sat down on a chair in the hallway. He twisted and turned and tried to see through the glass door. He untied both shoelaces and retied them. He pulled his knees up to his chest and stretched his T-shirt over them, then dropped his feet to the floor again. He listened to the names of doctors being called over the hall speaker and wondered if any were hurrying down to take care of Caroline.

At last a nurse came through the glass door. Wally leaped up.

"What happened?" he asked the nurse.

She stopped. "To whom?"

"Caroline Malloy! I saw them bring her in!" said Wally miserably.

"Is she a friend of yours?" asked the nurse.

"Yes," said Wally. "It . . . it wasn't dynamite, was it?"

"Dynamite?" the nurse said. "Of course not! Something fell on her at the school, and we don't get any answer at her house. Could you contact her parents for us?"

Something fell *on her?* Wally's feet felt as though they were stuck to the floor. He couldn't move! Caroline was dying and he had to go tell her mother?

Hi, Mrs. Malloy. I just came to tell you that Caroline is dying.

Hello, Mrs. Malloy. Your youngest daughter is dead.

Good afternoon, Mrs. Malloy. Well, it's not a good afternoon for you, anyway. In fact, it's probably the most awful afternoon of your life, because something fell on Caroline at the school and I'm here to deliver the sad news that your youngest daughter is no more. Passed on. Deader than a doornail.

No, this wouldn't do at all.

The nurse was looking at him strangely. "Would you possibly know where her parents are?"

Wally figured that Beth had gone to the baseball game to watch Eddie play, and Mrs. Malloy was probably off doing errands or something.

"I'll see if I can find her mom," Wally said.

"Tell her that Caroline wasn't seriously hurt, but school policy is to call an ambulance if someone has an accident on the premises. We'll probably take her up to X-ray, but we can't let her go home until a parent gets here."

So she *wasn't* dying!

Wally got back on his bike and headed for the road bridge leading to Island Avenue.

As he crossed the bridge, he saw Mrs. Malloy's car

ahead of him, just turning into the driv[e] Malloy house. Wally rode up behind her.

"Hello, Wally," Mrs. Malloy called, get[ting out of] her car and pulling two empty boxes from [the] seat. "How are you?"

"I'm fine, but Caroline's not," said Wally. "Something fell on her at the school and she's at the hospital."

"*What?*" cried Mrs. Malloy, dropping the boxes.

"She's okay, I think. But the nurse said for me to come and get you."

"What *happened*? Why was she at the school?" cried Caroline's mother.

"I don't know; I'm only the messenger," said Wally miserably.

Mrs. Malloy jumped back into the car and turned around so fast that she ran over one of the boxes. Soon the car was out of sight.

Wally rode down the hill to the swinging bridge and walked his bike across. Two more days and the Malloys would be gone. If he could just lie low for two more days—forty-eight hours—he could stop worrying that some terrible thing would happen and that he would be stuck with the Malloys forever.

Stranger things had happened. Suppose Mr. Malloy died of heatstroke in Ohio and Mrs. Malloy put the girls in the car to go home for the funeral and she was so upset that the car went off the bridge and the only person who survived was Caroline. And suppose his own mother said, "Poor Caroline! She has no one to take her in. We'll have to adopt her, and she can be your little sister, Wally. She'll be moving into your room and you can bunk with Peter."

Wally felt sort of sick. What if Caroline was hurt worse than the nurse thought? What if the X-rays showed that a broken bone had punctured her heart? What if she died here in Buckman and the Hatfords went to the funeral, and, because Wally had been in her class, he had to stand up in the front of the church and say nice things about her? What if he had to lie and say she was a true and loyal friend and her death left a hole in his heart forever?

Wally went into the house, lay down on the couch, and pulled a pillow over his head.

Nine

■

Oh, No!

There were no broken bones in Caroline's body, but Mrs. Malloy said she almost felt like breaking somebody's neck if anybody caused her any more trouble in the next two days. She said she didn't care if Caroline wanted to be onstage more than anything else in the world. Caroline ought to have had more sense than to go sneaking into a school where she shouldn't have been, and Mrs. Malloy told the girls' father this when he called to tell them that Ohio was really suffering in the heat wave.

"No more than we are here, George," she said. "It's so hot, I'm almost afraid to let Eddie play ball."

Nonetheless, she told him, as she had told the girls, the moving van was coming on schedule on Wednesday. It was due at eight in the morning, and as soon as all the furniture was out, she was turning the house over to a cleaning crew to get it ready for the Bensons' return. She and the girls had been invited to the Hatfords' for brunch before they left town, and wasn't that nice of Mrs. Hatford?

There was too much to do to even think about the Hatfords, and Caroline realized that perhaps they would see them for the last time on Wednesday and that would be that. Suddenly, after all the pranks and teasing and horseplay and fighting and laughing and swimming and walking to school together, it all would be over. *Poof!*

Beth was certainly happy. Her fantasy story about the Shanatee Indians had won second place in the library's short story contest. Eddie and Jake's team had tied for first place in summer baseball, and the league had called off the last game because of the heat.

But cars were pouring into Buckman from east and west and north and south because the college was celebrating its hundredth anniversary. For four days, every hotel, motel, boardinghouse, and bed-and-breakfast was full, not a single room available within thirty miles of Buckman. There were very few parking spaces as well.

"It's a good time to be getting out of town," Mrs. Malloy said to her girls. "If your father were still working for the college, I'd have to go to every tea and dinner and concert there was. I've never been so glad to go around in shorts and sandals as I am now. We're leaving town just in time."

Caroline tried to stay out of trouble. Her mother

did not need one more aggravation, that was certain. The heat made everyone short-tempered and miserable, so people tended to stay indoors in air-conditioning. This, of course, meant that they had more opportunity to get in each other's way.

The Hatford boys did not come over, and the Malloy girls did not go over to the boys' house. No one mentioned the old coal mine, and that was just as well. The swinging bridge between them remained deserted, as the muddy river beneath it moved sluggishly downstream.

Moving day arrived. The big Mayflower truck slowly backed into the driveway, and as Caroline watched from her window, three burly men got out and walked across the yard to the front door.

"Ready to go," Mrs. Malloy said, opening the door wide. "Everything's in boxes except the furniture."

It was a surprise to Caroline how fast the movers worked. The couch and the dining room table went first; then the beds were dismantled and carried out. One by one the rooms were emptied, until the girls' voices echoed around the house.

The rug, the dresser, the chairs, the lamps, the chests, and boxes, boxes, boxes . . .

And finally . . . the house was empty.

"Okay, lady, we'll see you in Ohio," the driver said.

"Be careful with my dishes," Mrs. Malloy told them. "Some of those belonged to my grandmother."

"We'll be as careful as if your grandmother herself was in those boxes," the driver said.

Mrs. Malloy and her daughters watched the big truck roll slowly down the driveway, then turn onto the road and start across the bridge.

"Are you ready to say goodbye to Buckman?" Mrs. Malloy asked. "Ready to tell the boys goodbye?"

"I was ready to tell them goodbye the day we moved in," said Eddie.

"I don't believe that for one minute," said her mother.

They were just walking out to the car when the cleaning crew arrived with buckets and mops and brooms and vacuum cleaners. Mrs. Malloy drove the car over the bridge to the business district, then turned onto College Avenue and drove to the Hatfords' house.

"I'll bet this is the last parking space in Buckman," she said, pulling up in front. "Did you *see* all those cars in town just now? This is the biggest crowd this college has ever had. It's nice of Mrs. Hatford to invite us for brunch. I doubt that we could have found a seat in any restaurant in town."

Mrs. Hatford met them at the door. "Hello, Jean," she said warmly. "Come on in, girls. Tom says he's sorry he'll miss you, but he's working today, of course. Please come and sit down at the table. I know you're anxious to get on the road, but we're so glad to have this little time with you."

The Hatford boys were standing awkwardly around the dining room, arms dangling at their sides. There was a platter of doughnuts in the center of the table, surrounded by plates of fruit and sausages and applesauce and scrambled eggs.

"You're so nice to do this, Ellen," said Mrs. Malloy. "I'll bet we'd find a waiting line all up and down the highway. We didn't eat much breakfast, and this looks delicious!"

Everyone took a seat at the table. Caroline had never seen her older sisters so tongue-tied. She was quiet herself, and the Hatford boys were practically speechless. They'd not had much trouble teasing and quarreling during the past year, but now that it was time for goodbyes, and mothers were present, no one quite knew what to say.

"We're going to miss you, aren't we, Wally?" Mrs. Hatford said.

Wally didn't answer.

"*I'll* miss them!" said Peter, having gratefully accepted the bag of cookies Beth had made just for him.

"So will Jake and Josh and Wally," said his mother.

"And the girls are going to find it really boring in Ohio without the boys," said Mrs. Malloy.

The girls didn't answer. The doughnuts went around a second time. So did the sausages and eggs. The boys were occupied with stuffing their faces, and only the two mothers seemed to find anything to talk about.

Mrs. Hatford was offering more juice when the phone rang, and she answered.

"Of course!" she said. "Yes, she's right here." She handed the phone to Mrs. Malloy. "It's your husband."

"George?" Mrs. Malloy got out of her chair and stood holding the telephone. "Hello?" she said. There was a pause. "What?" An even longer pause. "Oh, *no!*" she said.

Caroline stopped chewing and watched her mother. She most certainly looked worried, and that worried Caroline. "But we can't!" Mrs. Malloy was saying. "There's no place to go!" Beth and Eddie looked up.

Mrs. Malloy turned to Mrs. Hatford. "George tells me there's been a massive power outage in Ohio because of the heat. The electricity has been off in our county since nine last night, and now the power company says they don't think they can get it restored for three or four days!"

"Oh, my goodness!" said Mrs. Hatford.

Mrs. Malloy turned to the phone again. "George, every hotel here is booked solid! Every motel for fifty miles or more is full!"

Another pause. Then Mrs. Malloy spoke to her daughters. "He says it would be foolish to go home. There's no electricity, no air-conditioning, no traffic lights or streetlights. Even supermarkets and restaurants are shutting down because there's no refrigeration. I don't know what we're going to do!"

"There's only one thing *to* do, Jean," said Mrs. Hatford. "You're simply going to stay with us."

Ten

■

Moving Out

Their mother might as well have told them that the basement was flooded or the roof was on fire, Wally thought. She had to be half out of her mind. The heat had affected her, too! There was no place for the Malloys to sleep! No way could they fit four more people into their house!

He looked at his brothers. Jake and Josh were thunderstruck, but Peter grinned happily at the prospect.

"Oh, Ellen, how could you possibly put us up?" Mrs. Malloy protested.

"Where there's a will, there's a way. You'd do the same for me," Mrs. Hatford said. "There's no sense in your starting out with no idea where you'll spend the night or how long you'll have to be there. At least the kids know each other, and they can play outside. . . ."

Mrs. Malloy spoke into the telephone again. "Ellen

has invited us to stay here till we get our power back, George. . . . Yes, I know. . . . It's a great imposition on them, but I don't know what else to do. . . . Yes. . . . All right. . . . Yes, I will."

When she hung up the phone, she said, "You're an angel of mercy, Ellen. George says he'll call the minute the power comes back on, but almost the whole state is shut down, and so are parts of Pennsylvania and New Jersey."

"We're glad to have you here," Mrs. Hatford said. "Now we'll just figure out where everyone will sleep."

"Mo . . . ther!" Jake said earnestly in a low voice.

Mrs. Hatford ignored the protest. "The twins have the largest bedroom, so I think I'll put the four of you in there. They have twin beds, and I'll get an air mattress that sleeps two that we can squeeze onto the floor."

"That will be absolutely fine," said Mrs. Malloy.

"Mo-ther!" said Jake in despair. "What about *us*?"

"One of you boys can take your sleeping bag into Wally's room, and the other can sleep in Peter's," Mrs. Hatford said.

Wally tried to imagine the Malloys living in their house. "There's . . . there's only one bathroom! For ten people!" he choked.

"Plus the powder room here on the first floor. We'll make do. There just won't be any long showers, that's all. In fact, you boys may want to forget showers for a day or two," his mother said.

That was fine with Wally. But the thought of

waiting in line to use the toilet, and everybody knowing what you were waiting for, did not appeal to Wally at all. Jake and Josh were still in shock.

"They'll sleep in our beds!" Wally heard Jake whisper.

"They'll look in our closet!" Josh whispered back.

Wally glanced across the table at Caroline, Beth, and Eddie. They didn't seem any happier about it than his brothers were.

"Okay," said Mrs. Hatford determinedly. "We're going to make this as painless as possible, and who knows? Maybe it will be fun!"

Like going to the dentist is fun, Wally thought.

"We'll do all we can to help," said Mrs. Malloy.

"Jake and Josh," said their mother, "go get some of your clothes to wear for the next few days. Take your sleeping bags, too. They're in your closet. And a few games might be nice. Wally and Peter, go to your rooms and make sure everything's off the floor so the twins can put down their sleeping bags."

Like robots—all but Peter, who practically skipped to the stairs—the boys rose from their chairs and started toward the hall.

"I'm so sorry to impose like this," Wally heard Mrs. Malloy say. "I know how the kids must hate it."

"It's not much trouble, really!" said Mrs. Hatford.

She lies, Wally thought.

At the top of the stairs, Jake said, "This can't be happening! It's my worst nightmare! *Worse* than my worst nightmare! Eddie will be sleeping in my bed! I'll have

67

to decontaminate it, practically, before I can sleep in it again."

"I'm taking my own pillow," said Josh. "I don't want anyone sleeping on my pillow."

"I'm not sleeping in Peter's room, either," said Josh. "Wally, you can sleep in Peter's room and Jake and I will take yours."

This always happened. Wally had known it would happen. But he opened his mouth and said, "No way."

"What do you mean?" said Jake.

"*N* as in *noodle* and *O* as in *Oreo*," said Wally. "It's my room and I'm sleeping in my own bed." There. He'd said it. Jake looked like he might punch him in the mouth, but he didn't.

"Well, then we're both going to sleep on your floor," Jake said. "We'll put all our stuff in Peter's room, but we're not sleeping in separate bedrooms."

"Okay by me," said Wally. *Amazing how great you feel when you stand up for yourself,* he thought.

He went into his room and kicked all the extra stuff under his bed. The worn underwear, the new sneakers, the *National Wildlife* magazine, the kickball . . . Then he went across the hall and stood in his brothers' doorway, watching them yank stuff out of their desk drawers before the girls got upstairs.

"Don't let them see any old papers!" said Josh.

"Don't let them see any school stuff at all," said Jake.

"Look at this!" Josh said, holding up a picture he had drawn in kindergarten—a boy with a head as big as a pumpkin and a strange smile on his face. There must have been dozens more, all crammed into a bottom drawer.

"And this!" said Jake, checking his middle desk drawer. There was a report card from second grade, and the teacher had written at the bottom, *Jake could be a better student if he tried, but his temper and impulsiveness sometimes get in the way.*

"You'd better take that along," said Josh. "Who knows what else you've got in your desk? Probably something even worse."

"We should move the desks!" Jake said in despair. He was busy loading up his arms. "Take any money you've got lying around—all your state quarters, Josh. Your stamp collection, too."

"And don't forget all your baseball caps," said Josh. "Eddie would love to get her hands on those."

They grabbed jeans and shorts from their closet, then pushed the remaining clothes as far back in the corner as possible, so that the girls' clothes wouldn't touch theirs when they hung them up.

There were footsteps on the stairs, and the twins left their bedroom just as Mrs. Malloy and Mrs. Hatford appeared at the top.

"Let me help you with the sheets," Mrs. Malloy said.

"If you'd like," said Mrs. Hatford, taking a stack of pillowcases out of the closet and handing them to the girls' mother. "If you could put fresh sheets on the beds in the twins' room, I'll make sure we have plenty of towels in the bathroom."

Wally and his brothers fled back downstairs and

found themselves alone with the Malloy girls in the kitchen.

"Talk about a bummer!" Eddie said at last.

"I'd rather turn over my room to a hippopotamus," said Jake.

"Thanks for nothing," said Eddie.

"Are you guys going to start fighting again?" asked Peter from the doorway, his hands on his hips. "*I* think this could be fun!"

Everyone looked at Peter as though he had just stepped out of a spaceship. Fun? Having girls in their bedroom? Using the same bathroom, too? Having to get up in the morning and face each other across the breakfast table?

But there was some truth in what Peter was saying, Wally had to admit. The chief offenders were Jake and Eddie. As long as they were fighting, it was hard for anyone else to get along.

Eleven

■

Stop Complaining!

"Well, I guess we're stuck," Beth said. "We'll have to make the best of it."

"Yeah!" said Peter. "No more fighting!"

"So who's fighting?" asked Jake. "I just don't want them sleeping in my bed, that's all."

"Don't worry," said Eddie. "I wouldn't sleep in your bed for a million dollars. I'll be on the air mattress, you can bet."

"It must be awful at home," said Beth. "Mom said Dad told her it was ninety-six degrees in our upstairs. By tomorrow, all the food in the refrigerator will be spoiled. Ugh."

"It's supposed to be a hundred and four here tomorrow," said Josh. "What are we going to do today?"

"We could trap flies in the sun and put a magnifying glass on them and watch them go crazy," said Eddie.

"That's cruel!" Caroline declared. "Besides, I don't want anything to do with bugs."

"At least we can go swimming if it gets unbearable," said Beth.

"Not!" said Eddie. "We packed our bathing suits, remember. We thought we'd be home by tonight."

"I know!" said Peter. "We could make peanut butter and banana milk shakes! And bake cookies!"

"It's too hot for cookies, Peter," said Beth.

"We could take Caroline's school picture and make copies of it at the library and turn them into Wanted posters at the post office," said Jake.

"Not!" said Caroline.

"We could make lemonade and sell it at a stand out front," Beth suggested.

"We've tried that, but people don't come down our block much," said Wally. "Monopoly?"

"Bor-ing!" said Eddie.

What happened was that when the bedrooms were finally ready, with sleeping bags on the floor of Wally's room, fresh sheets on the beds in the twins' bedroom, and an air mattress there on the floor, the girls shut themselves up in the boys' bedroom for the afternoon, sprawled out on the beds, with books and magazines for company, and Wally and his brothers spent the afternoon on the porch.

By five o'clock, Mrs. Malloy insisted that the girls come downstairs and be sociable. And if they couldn't be sociable, she said, they could at least ask Mrs. Hatford what they might do to be helpful.

"Well, you could set the table for dinner," Mrs.

Hatford replied. "Your mother and I have been cooking extra meals, because I have to go back to work tomorrow. Hopefully, even if it gets hotter here in Buckman, we'll have enough food prepared that we won't have to use the oven again for several days."

"What if it turns out we can't go home for a week, Mother?" Eddie said worriedly.

"I doubt it will be a week," Mrs. Malloy told her. "I called your father this afternoon, and he said the power company hopes to have power restored to all of Ohio in four days at the most."

Four days! thought Caroline. Four days of lying in a room at the Hatfords' was like a prison sentence. But she took the handful of silverware Mrs. Hatford gave her and dutifully walked around the dining room table, placing the knives and forks beside each plate.

When Mr. Hatford walked in at six, the shirt of his postal uniform was drenched in perspiration, and he had a small towel draped around his neck. He stopped and stared at the Malloys in surprise.

"Well," he said. "Hello."

"Tom, we've got a little emergency here," his wife told him. "George called to say that there's a huge power outage in Ohio due to the heat. No electricity, no traffic lights or refrigeration or air-conditioning. There's no use in Jean and the girls going home to that, and no hotel here for them to go to. So I've invited them to stay with us for a few days until they get their power back."

Mr. Hatford blinked. Caroline supposed he wasn't

any happier about it than the boys had been. "Well," he said. "Any port in a storm, right?"

"We are so grateful for Ellen's invitation, but we know this is an imposition," Mrs. Malloy said. "We're going to be as helpful as possible, and I've made a couple of lemon pies. I hope that will make up for it a little."

Mr. Hatford laughed. "Well, now, I don't have any objection to that!" he said. "Yes, I heard about that power outage in Ohio. Pretty serious, I understand." Turning to his wife, he said, "I need to take a shower before dinner." And then, "I *can* take a shower?"

"Yes. We've talked about conserving the hot water," Mrs. Hatford said, and Mr. Hatford headed for the stairs.

■

Dinner helped perk everyone up. It was a cold meal of tuna and macaroni salad, with homemade rolls, sliced tomatoes, corn on the cob, and Mrs. Malloy's lemon pies.

The adults did most of the talking, with Mr. Hatford telling about how crowded it was in town with so many alumni returning for the college's anniversary—how impossible it was to drive around campus delivering mail with cars parked all over the place, mostly where they shouldn't be.

After the meal was over, the girls did the dishes while the adults sat in the living room watching the evening news.

"Three-fourths of the state of Ohio has been affected

by the current power failure," the announcer said. "Crews are working around the clock, but the governor has said there is still no clear idea of when all communities will have power. Generators are being set up in gymnasiums where citizens with health risks may go to cool off, but travelers are urged to stay out of Ohio until the crisis is over."

Caroline and her sisters joined the Hatford boys on the porch when the kitchen was clean. The next night it would be the boys' turn to clean up. Mrs. Malloy had talked them into doing the dishes by hand to save the hot water for showers. It almost seemed to Caroline as though her own mother was trying to make things as difficult as possible.

The boys had taken over the rocking chair and the glider, so Caroline, Beth, and Eddie sprawled on the steps. Caroline thought the boys did look a little smug, having escaped kitchen duty this time, their stomachs full of lemon pie.

Instead of saying something pleasant to the girls, Jake said, "Too bad the power didn't go out when you were halfway back to Ohio. Your dad *would* have to call while you were still here!"

"Yeah? I don't know what *you're* complaining about," said Eddie. "You've got free maid service. We did the dishes, remember."

"Hey, you guys," said Josh. "You know what I think? I think you two ought to go hide in a cave or something till the heat wave's over. I'm tired of hearing you gripe at each other all the time. I mean it."

"I am too!" said Beth. "Nobody likes that we have to be here, you know."

Jake and Eddie looked quickly around at the others, surprised, it seemed, that their own brothers and sisters were turning against them.

"I just wish there was something exciting to do," said Eddie. "We never did go to the old coal mine. I'm going to go up there and look around."

"Yeah? I dare you," said Jake.

"I dare you *both*!" said Josh. "Maybe that'll stop your complaining."

And Caroline knew that a dare, to Eddie, was as good as a done deal.

Twelve

■

Undercover Operation

Wally did not know when anything had felt weirder than having Eddie, Beth, and Caroline sleeping in his house. Here in the upstairs! In Jake and Josh's bedroom!

The twins had dumped all their stuff on the floor in Peter's room and were sprawled out now on their sleeping bags in Wally's room. But those sleeping bags alone took up most of the floor space. If Wally had to get up in the night, he'd have to take wide steps, putting his feet only on the places where there wasn't an arm or a leg.

"This stinks! They'll snoop through everything!" said Jake.

"I got most of the stuff out of our desks, though," said Josh. "I got the journal I was keeping for a while, and all your baseball cards."

Suddenly Jake gave a little cry and bolted upright. "Our underwear!" he gasped. "We didn't clean out the dresser! We left our underwear!"

Wally watched as Jake fell back on his sleeping bag, eyes closed. For once something humiliating was happening to Wally's brothers, not to him. He imagined Caroline coming down to breakfast in the morning with Jake's underpants on her head. He imagined Eddie going out to his mother's vegetable garden in the backyard and picking tomatoes for lunch, using Josh's underwear for a basket. He imagined Beth fastening little pink bows to the front of each pair.

"Man oh man!" he said, trying not to laugh. "That could be embarrassing."

"We've got to get them out of there!" said Josh.

"The girls?" asked Wally.

"The underwear!" Jake and Josh howled together.

"What are you going to do? Sneak in there while they're asleep?" asked Wally. "Everyone's gone to bed."

"I don't know. We'll think of something," said Jake, and who knew what that something would be?

It had been a hot, miserable day, made worse by Wally's brothers' taking up all his floor space with their sleeping bags, and all the air with their complaints—Jake's in particular. Not only that, but their shoes stank! All Wally wanted to do was fall asleep and forget how many people were in his house just now.

Once, in the night, Wally had to go to the bathroom. He did not want to go out into the hall and bump into a Malloy girl. Maybe he could hold it in till morning, he thought. He turned onto his left side. He turned onto his right. He couldn't hold it in much longer.

Finally he got out of bed, edged his way around his brothers, and slowly opened his bedroom door so that it wouldn't creak. Then, in his tiger pajamas, he stepped out into the hall and took a step toward the bathroom. There, coming straight toward him, was Caroline Malloy in her Little Mermaid pajamas. A tiger and a mermaid did not mix at all.

He knew that Caroline, being a guest, should be allowed to go to the bathroom first. But Wally's feet kept moving. He made it two steps ahead of Caroline. He slipped inside and locked the door. When he was through, he drank half a glass of water, being careful not to touch any glass that the Malloys might have used. Then he opened the door, and there was Caroline with her arms folded, listening to everything.

Back in his room again, Wally pulled the covers over his head and tried to count the number of days, hours, minutes, seconds that the Malloys might be in his house.

He must have dropped off to sleep, because the next thing he knew, Jake was shaking his arm.

"Wally," Jake kept whispering. "Wally . . ."

"Huh?" Wally murmured, rolling over.

"Listen. We need you to do something."

"Huh?" Wally said again. He had that sinking feeling. Josh was awake too, and they were both looking at him.

"We need you to sneak into our bedroom and scoop up all our underwear from the dresser."

"No!" said Wally. "No! No! No!"

"Your feet are smaller," Josh explained. "You can creep around that room easier than we can with our big feet. We'd probably step on someone. It's four in the morning. They're all asleep."

"No! Do it yourself! It's *your* underwear!" said Wally.

"Walll-ly," said Josh. "Do you remember those underpants Grandma sent you for your birthday last year? The ones with your name on the seat?"

"Yes . . . ," Wally said, beginning to see where this conversation was going.

"And you know how Mom gets our underwear mixed up sometimes when she does the laundry? Well, if the Malloys see *our* underwear, they won't know exactly who it belongs to, Jake or me. But if they see any with *Wally* on them, they'll know for sure."

Wally closed his eyes, but it didn't keep out the pictures. A picture of Eddie riding around town on one of the Hatfords' bikes, with Wally's underwear flying from the handlebars. Beth using a pair of Wally's underpants as a book cover. Caroline coming to breakfast with a hat made out of underwear, with *Wally* across her forehead. He couldn't stand it.

"Where *is* your underwear?" he asked.

"The bottom drawer," said Jake. "Just softly open our door, tiptoe around the air mattress, pull out the bottom drawer of our dresser, and scoop up all the stuff. Then bring it back here. That's all you have to do."

All he had to do. It was like asking him to climb Mount Everest and be back by sundown.

Wally got out of bed. He walked to the door.

"Goodbye," he said to his brothers, because if Mrs. Malloy and her daughters found him creeping around their bedroom at four in the morning, he might not live to see the next day.

He padded down the hall. Gently, gently, he opened the door of the twins' room. He waited, holding his breath, while he took in the room, trying to see where everyone was sleeping. Carefully, carefully, Wally made his way around the air mattress with Caroline and Eddie on it, around the bed where Beth was lying, around the other bed, where Mrs. Malloy lay sleeping, one arm dangling over the edge, and over to the dresser along the far wall.

Slowly, slowly, Wally stooped down and, feeling around, put his hands on the two knobs of the bottom drawer, then slowly, slowly—so it wouldn't make a sound—pulled it open.

Again he held his breath and waited, sure that any minute Mrs. Malloy would rise and say, "Just what do you think you're doing in our room, young man?" Or that his dad would see the door open and thunder, "Wally, what the heck are you doing in there?"

But no one spoke. No one stirred. Taking a deep breath, Wally put his hands in the drawer, one at each end, and scooped up all the underwear. Now he'd be discovered for sure. Once again, however, no one stirred. With his right foot he softly edged the drawer closed. Wally turned slowly around. Step by step . . . Pause . . . Breathe . . . Step by step . . . Pause . . . Breathe . . .

He reached the door. Still no sound. This was too easy. Things never turned out this well for Wally Hatford. Something always *had* to go wrong. It was inevitable.

He stepped out into the hall. Transferring all the underwear to one arm, he used his other hand to softly close the door behind him. He went down the hall to where Jake and Josh were waiting for him. They pulled him into the bedroom and closed the door behind him.

"Way to go, Wally!" said Jake.

"You did it!" said Josh. "Wally, you're the best! Did you get it all?"

"Yep," said Wally, scarcely believing it. Now he almost *hoped* there was a pair of his underpants mixed up with theirs so that he could feel double the relief. Jake turned on the light. The boys stared.

There on the floor was a pile of girls' underwear. Underpants with daisies on them. One pair that said *Monday* and another that said *Friday.* There were pink underpants with hearts, and blue underpants with stripes. And even a pair that read *Caroline* on the seat.

Thirteen

■

The Magic Underwear

A shaft of sunlight fell on Caroline's face. It was the heat more than the light that woke her, for the sun was already hot. She yawned and rolled over, then opened her eyes and stretched.

Now she remembered. She was beside Eddie on an air mattress on the floor in the Hatford boys' bedroom.

Well, she certainly didn't want to lie here all day, and besides, she was hungry. She wondered what Mrs. Hatford might have left for their breakfast before she went to work. Maybe she could get the others to go to the ice cream store for cones before the day got too hot.

She sat up and looked around. Her mom and her two sisters were still asleep. Maybe it wasn't as late as she thought. Caroline slipped off her pajamas and pulled open the bottom drawer of the dresser, where the girls had put their things after they'd thrown the boys' stuff in the closet.

Empty! The drawer was empty! How could that be? Maybe Eddie had moved their clothes somewhere. But why would she do that?

"What's the matter, Caroline?" came her mother's sleepy voice from one of the twin beds.

"All our underwear's gone!" said Caroline, puzzled, pulling on her pajamas again.

"What?" murmured Beth.

"Gone!" said Caroline. "Our underwear's gone."

Eddie rose on one elbow. *"What?"* she cried. And together the girls gasped, "The boys!"

"The boys stole your *underwear?*" said their mother in disbelief.

"Ha!" said Eddie. "They'd steal our teeth and our toenails if they could. They'd steal the hair off our heads if we'd let them."

"But I can't imagine those boys coming into our bedroom while we were sleeping and taking our *underwear!*" said Mrs. Malloy, sitting up. "I'm sure they weren't raised to do something like that."

"I think you should call their mom at the hardware store and tell her," said Caroline.

"Now, look!" said Mrs. Malloy. "The Hatfords are graciously letting us stay in their house until we can go home. We are not going to say one word about this to the parents. I'll handle it myself."

Everyone got dressed, wearing underpants from the day before, and found Jake and Josh and Peter sitting quietly at the kitchen table, eating their cereal.

"Good morning, boys," said Mrs. Malloy. "Where's Wally this morning?"

"He's feeling sort of sick," said Peter.

"Oh? What's wrong?" asked Mrs. Malloy.

"He's sick to his stomach," said Peter.

Just then, however, Wally came in and, without a word, sat down at the table and reached for the cereal. He did look a little sick, as though he'd been outside throwing up.

"Good morning, Wally," said Eddie, Beth, and Caroline together.

"Hi," Wally mumbled.

"I see that your mom left us some of her delicious banana bread," said Mrs. Malloy. "That's a favorite of mine." She reached for the pitcher of orange juice and poured a glass for herself. "I just want to say, boys, that some things are missing from our bedroom, and I would like them to be returned immediately."

Caroline looked across the table at the boys. They were sitting like frogs, she thought, their eyes huge. They didn't blink. They didn't even appear to be breathing.

Peter, however, got up from the table and went upstairs. His brothers stared after him. The girls stared too.

Peter? Caroline wondered. *Peter* Hatford had stolen into their room the night before and taken their underpants? There were footsteps on the stairs again, and Peter came back down. He walked over to Mrs. Malloy and placed a Snickers wrapper and a Tootsie Roll wrapper on the table in front of her.

Mrs. Malloy stared at the wrappers, then at Peter. "What are these?" she asked.

"Some things I took from the room," said Peter.

"When?" asked Mrs. Malloy.

"Last week," said Peter.

"Aha!" said Jake. "*You're* the one who ate my candy!"

"I'm not talking about candy, boys," said Mrs. Malloy. "Someone must have come into our bedroom last night and taken clothes that didn't belong to him. We want them back."

Jake and Josh and Wally looked at each other and shrugged.

"Okay, come with me," said Mrs. Malloy. "All of you."

Everyone got up from the table and followed her upstairs.

"Caroline," her mother said. "Show us what you found this morning."

With everyone watching, Caroline walked over to the dresser and pulled open the bottom drawer. There were the girls' underpants. She stared, wide-eyed, then turned to her sisters in disbelief.

"I thought you said it was empty!" said her mother.

"It *was*! There weren't any underpants here at all!" Caroline declared.

"Now, Caroline . . . ," said her mother, frowning.

"Mom, the bottom drawer was empty!" Caroline protested. "I *know* that's where we put our stuff."

"Boys," said Mrs. Malloy. "I'm sorry, but I think the heat's beginning to get to Caroline and we jumped to conclusions. I'm sorry I interrupted your breakfast. Let's all go back down and forget this ever happened."

"Good idea!" said Jake.

Caroline could not believe this! No! She had opened the drawer with her own two hands and seen with her own two eyes that it was empty! She had *not*, however, shown it to Beth or Eddie or their mom. She had only told them about it. Now the drawer was full again. Was she losing her mind?

Maybe after a whole year of living near the Hatfords, she was slowly going crazy. And then Caroline did what she always did when faced with something difficult. *Remember this,* she told herself, because when she became a famous actress on Broadway, she would know how it felt to slowly lose one's mind, and she would be able to play the part well.

At breakfast Jake and Josh and Wally sat across the table from her with mouths as straight as rulers, but their eyes, she knew, were laughing. If she had ever seen laughing eyes in her life, these were the eyes.

Only Peter had a puzzled expression on his face, and Caroline almost felt sorry for him—having to live with those three conniving brothers of his!

The girls went straight up to their room after breakfast while Mrs. Malloy straightened the kitchen and read over Mrs. Hatford's notes about what there was for lunch and what they might prepare for dinner. The problem with being a grown-up, Caroline decided, was that you always had to think about food if you were the cook. No sooner was breakfast over than you had to start planning lunch. No sooner was lunch over than you had to think about dinner. She hoped that when she became an actress on Broadway, she would be rich enough to eat in hotels for the rest of her life.

"They tricked us, all right," said Eddie. "I'll bet that after we went down to breakfast, Wally put our underwear back."

"Obviously," said Beth.

The sun was shining through the windows, and it was getting warmer by the minute. The girls didn't want to stay up in the bedroom all day.

"*Ring!*" Eddie commanded the downstairs phone. "Please ring and say we can go home."

But the phone did not ring, and as the day grew hotter still, the sounds of traffic increased. More and more cars were coming to Buckman for the college anniversary.

"They're even parking way back here!" said Beth, watching the steady stream. "I'll bet you can't get *near* the college!"

"Hey," said Eddie. "Look what the Stupids are doing!"

Caroline went over and looked out the window at the Hatford boys on the sidewalk. She couldn't tell what they were doing, but they didn't look stupid. "Why do you have to call them that?" she asked.

"Yes," said Beth. "It's boring, Eddie, the way you're always tearing them down."

Eddie stared at them. "I can't *believe* you two! The Hatfords are our mortal enemies. Why are you sticking up for them?"

"We're going to miss them and you know it," said Beth. "Couldn't we just for one day—one hour—one *minute*—act like we're friends?"

"With Jake? Are you kidding?" said Eddie.

"Anyway," said Beth, "what *are* they doing?"

The girls watched some more. Josh was unfolding the legs of a card table, and Peter was setting out paper cups.

"They must be setting up a lemonade stand," said Caroline. "That's got to be it."

But Wally and Jake appeared to be getting ready to do something else, and the only thing for the girls to do was go outside and find out what.

■ ■ ■ ■ ■ ■ ■ ■ ■ ■ ■

Fourteen

■

Eggs-actly!

Wally felt on top of the world. After breakfast, when the boys went back to his room, he pointed to their underwear, piled in the corner.

"Good *show,* Wally!" Jake said, slapping him on the back.

"Nice *going*!" said Josh. "*That's* using your head!"

"But where did you find it?" asked Jake.

"The closet," said Wally. "They'd just thrown them there on the floor."

"What dorks!" said Jake, even though the under-wear in question was now in a heap on *Wally's* floor. "Man, will I ever be glad when they're gone."

"Oh, you will not," said Josh. "When did we ever have this much fun with the Bensons?"

"Plenty of times," said Jake. "When the Bensons come back, I'll forget the Malloys even existed."

"Boy, it's hot today!" said Wally, staggering about the bedroom a bit. "It's so hot, I'm going to try to fry an egg on the sidewalk."

He could not believe he had said that. Most of the time, when Wally said his ideas out loud, it only made his brothers tease him. But this time he had said it with such conviction that he had made it sound like a really good idea. But what *else* was there to do on a day when the temperature was supposed to reach a hundred and four?

Jake called the hardware store and talked to their mother. She said they could use the bag of lemons in the fridge if there was enough sugar in the pantry to make lemonade. There was, so Jake and Wally set to work squeezing lemons, and Josh made two signs. One read:

FRESH COLD ICED LEMONADE
$1.00 per cup

The other read:

WATCH US FRY AN EGG ON THE SIDEWALK
$1.00 if it works
Money back if it doesn't

Even Peter knew the risk in that.

"What if a dozen people want to see us fry an egg on the sidewalk and we use up a dozen eggs and it still doesn't work?" he asked.

91

"I don't know," said Wally. "I'll think of something." He was beginning to sound like his brothers! *So what's the worst that can happen?* he asked himself. Answer: he'd have to use his own money to buy his mom a dozen eggs. He could live with that.

They were putting up the signs when the girls came out on the porch.

"What's up?" called Beth.

"Going into business," said Wally.

"Lemonade, I'll bet," said Caroline.

"You got it," said Josh. "With all these people coming into Buckman on the hottest week in history and parking all the way down here, we could make a mint!"

But Eddie was looking at the other sign taped to a telephone pole near the sidewalk.

"You're actually going to try this?" she asked. "You're sure going to waste a lot of eggs."

"We'll see," said Wally.

When everything was ready, the seven kids sat on the front steps in the shade and hoped for the temperature to climb. Hot as it was, with the noon sun beating down heavily on the cement sidewalk, they wanted it hotter still. By one o'clock, Wally either saw or imagined he saw shimmering waves rise up from the hot concrete.

The morning events at the college must have been over, and people began streaming back toward their cars, ready to go somewhere for lunch.

A few bought lemonade, but almost everyone wanted to see Wally fry an egg on the sidewalk. The question was, should he charge every person who stopped to look, or only the person who did the asking first and paid the dollar? There was a lot to think about when you went into business for yourself.

Jake dashed inside the house and came out with his baseball cap, using it as a collection plate for dollar bills.

"Who wants to see?" he asked, passing the cap around. "Who wants to pay a dollar to see us fry an egg on the sidewalk?"

"I'll pay," a man said, smiling, "but make it snappy, because I'm about ready to fry here myself."

Jake managed to collect four dollars. The others just stood back, waiting, and Wally knew he had to act fast.

He opened the egg carton. He took out one big egg. Then he went to the hottest spot he could find on the sidewalk—a place where the sun had been beaming down all morning without shade. Squatting down with a flourish, Wally cracked the egg gently on the edge of the sidewalk, then held it up a few inches, broke the shell open, and let the yolk and the white fall out. *Splat!*

At first it appeared that nothing was happening. There certainly was no sizzle of fat or scent of bacon, the way there was when their mother cooked breakfast. Jake and Josh and Peter watched uneasily. The girls were grinning.

Then, slowly, the edges of the egg white began turning whiter. People began to smile. More people gathered to see what everyone was looking at. A couple more put dollar bills into the baseball cap.

"Hey! Look at that! Some kid's frying an egg on the sidewalk!" someone called out behind Wally.

"Well, I wouldn't call it fried, exactly, but I might call it poached," said a woman in a sundress.

A photographer who had been taking pictures at the college walked over. He edged his way through the crowd, saw the egg on the concrete, and immediately took a picture of Wally squatting over the cooking egg.

"Hey, I'll take mine sunny-side up," said a man, laughing.

"How about over easy?" said another.

"Do it, Wally!" said Peter. "Let's take orders and serve breakfast!"

People laughed. Some began turning away to find their cars, while still others came over to see what was going on. Cars were not only parked on the Hatfords' side of the street but all along the riverbank as well.

Wally took the kitchen spatula and tried to slip it under the egg. Part of the egg came up, but the rest didn't, and it slipped back onto the hot sidewalk, the yolk breaking.

"Here, let me do it!" said Jake, grabbing the spatula out of Wally's hand. "Who wants to try one? Who wants one over easy?" he called out. But Josh had the egg carton, and Jake tried to get it out of his hand. Suddenly *splat, splat, splat!*

The carton tipped over, out of their hands, and one after another the eggs fell on the hot cement.

"Scrambled eggs!" yelled Peter, and everyone laughed some more.

"Oh, boy, what a mess," one woman said as she turned to leave. "Good luck, guys."

"Look what you've done!" Jake yelled at Josh.

"*You* did it, not me!" said Josh.

Peter chortled, "Scrambled eggs! Come and get your hot scrambled eggs!"

"Shut up, Peter," said Jake.

Wally stood staring at the mess on the sidewalk. All the yolks had lost their shiny look and were beginning to turn dry. All the transparent whites of the eggs were turning opaque.

Now it was the girls, sitting on the steps, their mouths as straight as rulers, who were laughing with their eyes.

Mrs. Malloy came out on the porch to see what all the people were looking at. "What in the world . . . ?" she said. "Boys, did your mother say you could do that?"

Sure, thought Wally. *She said, "Take the eggs and go make a mess."*

"It's okay," said Josh. "We're cleaning it up."

"I certainly hope so," Mrs. Malloy said, and went back inside.

What Wally discovered was that eggs cooked without any grease stuck to the cement like paste. Digging as hard as he could with the spatula, he only got bits and pieces off. The cement had absorbed egg white like a sponge.

The twins finally brought out a bucket of soapy water and a brush and scrubbed down the sidewalk on their hands and knees. Wally poured himself a glass of lemonade and went up to drink it in the shade of the porch. Nothing could ruin his day! The big underwear switcheroo was about the best thing he'd done all summer, and the memory of that would last him a long time!

Fifteen

■

Seen!

The heat made everyone crabby. The next morning, Beth and Eddie both took their showers early, and there was no hot water left when Mr. Hatford rose to shower before work. The girls and their mother heard him grumbling in the hall.

"We are really getting in the way!" Mrs. Malloy said apologetically in the kitchen later.

"Now, Jean, you'd take us in too, and you know it," Mrs. Hatford assured her.

But afterward, as she was making the beds upstairs, Caroline's mother said, "I'd like to *think* I would be that neighborly if the Hatfords' power went out, but I'm afraid I'd think twice before I took in those four boys."

Jake and Eddie got into an argument. Mr. and Mrs. Hatford were at work, and Mrs. Malloy had put chicken salad and salami in the fridge for lunch.

However, Eddie took the last of the cheese, and this ticked Jake off.

"Hey, why didn't you take all the salami, too, while you were at it?" he groused.

"There were only two slices left," Eddie said.

"Yeah, one for you and one for somebody else," Jake told her. "Not two for you."

"Oh, shove it!" said Eddie. "You want some cheese?" She lifted the top piece of bread and yanked at a slice with a bite taken out of it. "Here's some cheese!" And she tossed it onto his plate.

"I don't want any cheese you've slobbered on," said Jake, throwing it back. It landed on the floor.

"Ewwww!" said Caroline.

"Now *no one* will want it!" Eddie snapped.

"Yeah. Serves you right for being a pig in the first place!" said Jake.

"Will you two stop arguing?" said Beth.

"Yeah, why don't you just go off and duke it out?" said Josh.

"Ha! Eddie wouldn't have a chance," said Jake.

"Go to the old coal mine!" Josh said, taunting. "Give you guys something to do besides fight." He stopped then. Caroline could tell he wished he'd never said it.

"*I'm* up for it!" said Jake. "*I'll* go!"

Caroline closed her eyes.

"Me too," said Eddie. She flashed a warning look at Beth and Caroline. "And don't tell Mom!" she added.

Caroline and Beth looked at each other. They saw the boys exchange nervous glances.

"So when are we going?" asked Jake.

"How about right now?" said Eddie.

"We shouldn't be *dooo-ing* this!" Peter sang.

"Just keep your mouth shut," said Jake. "Are we all in this together or what?"

"I'll go up there with you, but I'm not going in," said Wally.

"Okay by me," said Jake.

They all pulled on their sneakers.

"We're going out for a while, Mom," Eddie called up the stairs to her mother, who was making beds.

"Put on sunscreen if you're going to be out for long," Mrs. Malloy called back. "Will Peter be going with you?"

"Yes, we're taking him," called Wally.

They stuck to the trees when they could, to escape the broiling sun. Eddie and Jake led the way, their eyes steely, jaws clenched, each eager to show the other that they weren't afraid. Nobody said much as they trudged along.

When the low mountain loomed up at last, all Caroline could see was what appeared to be the entrance to a tunnel in its side.

"Is that it?" she asked Jake.

"Yeah," he said.

"Was it really a coal mine?" asked Beth.

"I don't know," said Josh. "Maybe it was a silver mine or lead or something. It's been closed for as long as I can remember."

"If Dad ever finds out we were up here . . . ," said Josh.

"So don't tell him! Nobody's going to get hurt. We're not going to do anything stupid," said Jake.

"Just coming up here was stupid," said Wally.

"So go home, then!" Jake growled, but nobody turned back.

There was a tall fence with barbed wire at the top surrounding the entrance to the mine, and every twenty feet or so, there was a NO TRESPASSING sign. But, as the kids soon discovered, the fence was in poor repair, and it did not take them long to see that if they jiggled and shoved at the gate, they could make the opening just wide enough for a person to slip through, providing that that person was a kid who held his breath and turned sideways.

"Listen, be careful," Beth warned as Eddie slipped through.

"Heck, nothing to it!" said Jake, going in after her.

The others watched uneasily from outside, holding on to the fence.

At first it appeared that Eddie and Jake were going to walk ten feet apart and not even speak to each other. But as they got closer to the tunnel, Caroline could see that they were at least talking. Now they were four feet apart . . . still talking. And finally they took a few steps together toward the tunnel entrance.

"Oh, man!" breathed Wally. "We don't even know what's in there."

"They'd better not fall in!" Peter said worriedly, his voice a little shaky. "We told Dad we wouldn't go in there, not ever, ever, ever."

"What if they go inside and it caves in on them?" said Caroline.

"That's why we're not supposed to go in," said Josh.

Jake and Eddie appeared to be thinking the same thing, because even after they reached the tunnel entrance, they both looked up and around, hesitant, it seemed, to go any farther.

Eddie turned to the others, by the fence, and waved.

Was this a final goodbye? Caroline wondered. Would this be the last memory she'd have of her sister? The weak smile, the wave from the entrance to the mountain, which at any moment could come roaring down onto her head?

Jake and Eddie started through the entrance, and then they disappeared.

Suddenly there was a shout. A yell. Popping up from brush at the side of the mountain was a big burly man in a dirty white T-shirt.

Jake and Eddie must not have got three feet inside before they came tearing out of the tunnel and almost collided with him. For a moment the man had Jake by the T-shirt, but Jake broke loose and he and Eddie ran pell-mell back down toward the gate.

"Get out!" the man yelled hoarsely. "Get out! You stay outta there. You get out of here and don't you never come back!"

He was twice their size, but Eddie and Jake were faster. On they ran, stumbling and tripping, the man in pursuit, until they reached the gate, white-faced and panting, and slipped through the opening. All the

Hatfords and Malloys ran like the wind, the man bellowing at them from the other side of the fence.

"I'll find you out; don't think I won't!" he shouted.

Caroline tripped and fell, but Beth yanked her up, and now they were far enough down the mountain that they could stop and catch their breath.

"*That* was close!" Eddie panted, holding her sides.

"Who do you suppose he was?" gasped Jake. "He just came out of nowhere!"

"He didn't have a uniform or anything," said Wally. "He didn't look like a guard."

"He looked half crazy to me," said Beth.

"Old Man of the Mountain!" said Josh. "Maybe he lives in there, like a troll or something."

"What do you think he would have done if he'd caught us?" Jake asked Eddie, still breathless.

"Arrested us, probably," said Eddie. "He didn't have a gun, did he?"

"I don't think so," Wally said.

"Should we sneak back up and try to figure out who he is?" Eddie asked.

"No!" all the others yelled. "Don't be crazy! We don't want him to know who *we* are either."

"Oh, man!" Wally said again. "If Dad ever found out . . ."

"If Mom knew I went inside . . . ," said Eddie.

As they made their way back across the field leading to the woods, an old rusty pickup truck came rolling down the overgrown path from the coal mine, turned away from the kids, who had ducked down in the tall grass, and headed for the road beyond.

"Was that him?" whispered Josh.

"I think so," said Jake. "I didn't get a really good look."

"How do you suppose *he* got inside the fence?" asked Eddie.

"Probably some back gate we don't know about," said Jake. "I hope he didn't figure out who we were."

Caroline knew that if their mother found out they had gotten into trouble—as though having to stay at the Hatfords' wasn't trouble enough—there would be no end of scolding that night, squeezed as they were in the twins' bedroom.

From the looks on the boys' faces—Josh's in particular—Caroline could tell that they were thinking the same thing about their father. He would probably say that maybe Eddie didn't know any better than to go into that old mine tunnel, but the boys certainly did, having lived their whole lives in Buckman.

"What did you see in the tunnel?" Caroline asked finally, as they started back toward the house.

"It was pretty dark," said Jake.

"Yeah. We *think* there was a pit or something farther on. It looked like maybe it was boarded up, but we could hardly see a foot in front of us," Eddie told her.

"And then we heard all that yelling," said Jake. He looked around. "We're going to keep our mouths shut, right?" He was looking directly at Peter.

Peter nodded. "If Dad asks me if we were at the old coal mine, I'll say, '*What* old coal mine?' "

Jake rolled his eyes. "Yeah. Right."

■ ■ ■ ■ ■ ■ ■ ■ ■ ■ ■ ■

Sixteen

■

Old Rusty Truck

Everyone was particularly well behaved at dinner that evening. Wally glanced around the table at the others. Jake and Josh, he knew, were hoping that the man at the mine had never seen them near their house and hadn't figured out who they were; hoping that the phone wouldn't ring, and that if it did, it wouldn't be the man telling their parents where they'd been. The girls, though, were probably hoping their dad would call from Ohio and say that they could come back home, that their power was on.

They gathered on the porch after dinner, and for the first time, Jake didn't dive for the glider and try to keep the Malloys from sitting on it.

"If nobody's reported us by now, then I don't think they're going to," he said. "That guy doesn't even know who we are."

"Well, *I'm* not gonna tell that we went to the coal mine," said Peter.

"Don't even *say* coal mine!" Jake warned.

"Then I won't even say that we went where we're not supposed to go, and besides, *I* didn't go in," said Peter.

"Don't even say *that*!" Jake told him. "Talk about ice cream or something."

The grown-ups came out on the porch after dinner just to see if it was cooling off any. The Malloy girls got up so that the parents could have the glider and the rocker.

"Doesn't seem like it's any cooler to me," Mrs. Hatford said. "I get so tired of being in air-conditioning all the time, but when I think of those poor folks in Ohio . . ."

"I sure wish I could carry some air-conditioning around with me on my deliveries," said Mr. Hatford. "I wouldn't mind that at all."

Mrs. Malloy fanned herself with the newspaper. "George called this afternoon and said the power company predicts it will have power restored to everyone by the end of the week."

"End of the *week*!" cried Caroline.

"He says it's an absolute mess. He had already stocked the refrigerator for our return, and now the milk has soured and everything has to be thrown out."

"Dry ice?" said Mr. Hatford.

"The city was giving it away, but now they've run out. They're busing senior citizens who live in apartments to community centers to keep cool, and all the public pools have issued free passes. Everyone's miserable, he says."

"Let's just hope we keep our power down here," said Mrs. Hatford. "Being in the mountains, West Virginia doesn't get as hot as Ohio generally, but this is as hot as I remember it ever being. How I wish this heat wave would break."

■

The next morning was even worse. When Wally woke, it was as though the sun had not set all night—as though it was just gathering energy to fry the whole state of West Virginia.

Mrs. Malloy offered to make French toast and bacon, but no one wanted anything hot. The seven kids sat listlessly at the kitchen table, pushing their cereal around in their bowls. Arms stuck to sides, thighs stuck to chairs, bare feet stuck to the floor, and the air conditioner was cooling only half as well as usual, because the power company was having a brownout to save fuel.

By noon, the heat outside had become almost unbearable. There was no breeze at all, and leaves hung lifelessly from the trees.

"I'm so hot, I could ignite," said Josh from the rocker.

Wally lay on his stomach on the porch floor and thought about that. He wondered if all the food he had eaten the night before could ever get so hot inside him that there would be spontaneous combustion. If he would just go *poof* and flare up from inside.

"I'm so hot, I could jump in the river with all my clothes on," said Beth.

"I dare you!" said Eddie.

"Me too!" said Caroline, standing up and kicking off her sandals.

And suddenly everyone was untying sneakers and leaving them in a pile on the porch. Jake jumped off the steps and led the way, and the seven kids swarmed down the bank below the swinging footbridge and sprawled belly first into the water.

It was the only place to be on a day like this. Wally felt his T-shirt cling to his chest, his shorts grow heavy over his hips. He flopped onto his back and let the slow current carry him a little downstream before he swam back.

Mrs. Malloy appeared at the top of the bank. "Who's watching Peter?" she called.

"I am," Josh answered. The rule was that nobody ever, ever went swimming without deciding first which twin—Jake or Josh—was lifeguarding Peter. Even though the water was scarcely waist deep in most places, except in the spring, that was the rule.

"I hope you girls realize you have only one set of clothes left. We didn't think we would be staying here," Mrs. Malloy said, laughing at the way they had jumped into the river wearing all but their shoes.

"We're too hot to care, Mom," Eddie called back.

"I know what you mean," Mrs. Malloy said. "I almost feel like jumping in myself."

When she went back into the house, Peter said, "I

don't need anyone to watch me. I'll be in third grade this fall."

"Yeah? I'll be going to middle school and I'll hardly know *any*one," said Eddie, swimming alongside him.

"Too bad you're not going into middle school here," Jake said. "We'd keep you company."

"Sure, you and your bag of tricks!" said Eddie.

"Hey!" said Wally, grabbing Josh's shoulder. "Look up there."

Going slowly along the road above was a rusty old pickup truck. The driver was looking down at the Hatfords and the Malloys splashing in the water.

"It's *him*!" breathed Eddie. "The man at the mine!"

"It's . . . it's like he's been looking for us!" said Wally.

The truck moved more and more slowly, until finally it came to a complete stop. The door opened. The driver got out. Six heads, all but Peter's, dived beneath the water.

Wally stayed under until he had no breath left. Gasping, he popped up to the surface, only to see the man standing up on the road beside his truck, arms folded across his chest. Under the water Wally went again.

The second time he and his brothers emerged, along with the Malloy girls, the man was getting back into his truck. He drove slowly away. But his face was turned toward the river.

"It *was* him!" said Caroline.

"And now he can guess where we live!" said Wally.

"Did he *say* anything to you, Peter, just now?" asked Jake.

"Huh-uh," said Peter.

"Did *you* say anything?" asked Josh.

Peter shook his head.

"You just stared at each other?" asked Eddie.

"We waved," said Peter. "Then he got back in his truck."

They didn't feel much like swimming anymore after that. They climbed back up the bank and stood wringing out their sopping wet clothes, then slogged their way across the road and up onto the Hatfords' porch.

Mrs. Malloy was reading the morning paper in the living room.

"Go change your clothes, and I'll wash the ones you were wearing," she told them. "And when you come back down, there's something in the paper you ought to see."

Jake stared at Eddie. Josh stared at Beth. Wally stared at Caroline.

But Peter trotted blissfully on upstairs, leaving wet footprints behind him.

"We're in for it now," Jake said when the boys were in Wally's room changing clothes, dropping their wet shorts and T-shirts on a towel on the floor. "I'll bet that guy reported us the other day—said he saw some kids at the mine. And now that he knows who we are, he's probably at the police station telling them where we live."

"What are you going to tell Dad when he finds out?" asked Wally. "He'll probably ground us for the rest of the summer."

"I don't know," said Jake. "The truth, I guess. Every time we lie, it only makes things worse."

They could hear Peter singing to himself in the next room as he changed clothes, then the Malloy girls going downstairs. Finally Jake and Josh and Wally went down to see what was in the newspaper.

"It's here on page three," Mrs. Malloy said, smiling.

And there it was—a picture of Wally Hatford frying an egg on the sidewalk.

■ ■ ■ ■ ■ ■ ■ ■ ■ ■

Seventeen

■

Once Upon a Midnight Dreary...

A breeze blew in that afternoon, and by five o'clock, the wind had picked up, and great rolling clouds came rushing from the west.

As Mrs. Malloy and Mrs. Hatford set to work making dinner, the boys' mother said, "I certainly hope this is a break in the heat and doesn't just pass us by. Sometimes after a rain, things are just stickier than they were before."

"Here, Caroline," Mrs. Malloy called. "You girls take this basket of corn out on the back porch and husk it so we can get it cooked before the power goes off."

"The power's going to go out here, too?" Caroline cried, a squeak in her voice.

"You never can tell," Mrs. Hatford said, turning over pieces of chicken that she was frying in the skillet.

"This summer has been a real drain on the power companies, and sometimes we're without power for a while."

Caroline could tell by the look on Wally's face that he was almost as horrified by the thought as she was. The Hatfords and the Malloys' sharing a house and a bathroom when the power was on was bad enough. The Hatfords and the Malloys with no power at all was too awful to contemplate.

Dinner went by without incident, however. The crunchy chicken and the mashed potatoes and gravy were devoured. The green beans and the sliced tomatoes and the steaming ears of yellow corn all disappeared in a hurry. There was even rhubarb pie for dessert, warm from the oven, with large dollops of vanilla ice cream melting on top of the sugary crust. Caroline would never tell her mother this, but she thought that Mrs. Hatford was about the most wonderful cook there was.

Toward the end of the meal, thunder rolled in like a freight train. Lightning preceded each boom, the crashes closer and closer together. The rain came in sheets, slashing hard against the windowpane.

About seven-thirty, when the plates had been stacked in the dishwasher, the refrigerator suddenly stopped humming and the lights went out.

"Oh, no!" came Mrs. Malloy's voice from the hall.

"Don't tell me!" said Mrs. Hatford.

The lights flickered on again, then went off. Everyone waited. They did not come back on.

"Better get the candles, Ellen," Mr. Hatford called. "I'll go light that kerosene lantern for the living room."

There was just enough evening light in the sky to maneuver around the house as the Hatford boys set candles here and there, making sure they were secure in their holders.

"You boys get some flashlights for the girls," said their dad.

"What about us?" asked Jake.

"You know this house better than they do. I think you can find your way around all right," said his father.

The boys grumbled a little, but they found small flashlights for all three girls, and soon candles flickered in the rooms downstairs, and moving circles of light traveled from room to room.

It was sort of exciting at first, but after an hour went by, then two, everything anyone wanted to do seemed to take twice as long—brushing teeth, working a puzzle, reading the comics. Without the air conditioner, the humidity seeped back into the house and the temperature rose.

"What we need is some entertainment," Mrs. Hatford said. "Tom, did anything exciting happen on your mail route today that you can tell us about?"

"Almost ran over a cow. Not much more than that," Mr. Hatford said from his recliner. "If Mr. Foster doesn't keep those cows penned, he's going to lose one, and somebody's going to have himself a steak dinner."

Though the worst of the rain had passed, the

lightning continued from time to time, and the thunder was like the low growl of a dog.

"Well, I think we need a little more to entertain us than a cow," Mrs. Hatford said. "Does anyone know a poem or something to recite for us?"

"Caroline knows some of 'The Raven,' by Poe," said Mrs. Malloy.

"By all means, let's hear it, Caroline!" Mrs. Hatford said. "It's been years since I've heard that poem."

"I remember reading it in high school," said Mr. Hatford.

Caroline looked around. This was for real. This was better than the boys asking for a poem. *She,* Caroline Lenore Malloy, was being called upon to give a presentation.

The boys started to clap. "Car-o-line! Car-o-line!" they chanted, even though she knew they didn't mean it.

Caroline stood up and went to stand by the kerosene lamp on the coffee table. She cleared her throat and then began in her best and spookiest voice:

> *"Once upon a midnight dreary,*
> *while I pondered, weak and weary,*
> *Over many a quaint and curious volume*
> *of forgotten lore—*
> *While I nodded, nearly napping,*
> *suddenly there came a tapping,*
> *As of someone gently rapping, rapping*
> *at my chamber door.*

‘ ’Tis some visitor,’ I muttered,
   ‘tapping at my chamber door—
Only this and nothing more.’ ”

Caroline used her hands to gesture toward the front door, and their movements made shadows dance on the walls. She continued:

"Ah, distinctly I remember it was in
   the bleak December,
And each separate dying ember wrought
   its ghost upon the floor.
Eagerly I wished the morrow;
   vainly I had sought to borrow
From my books surcease of sorrow—
   sorrow for the lost Lenore . . ."

Caroline pronounced the name clearly and distinctly, because she felt that Edgar Allan Poe had written this poem just for her. She placed her hand over her heart as she went on.

"For the rare and radiant maiden
   whom the angels named Lenore—
Nameless here for evermore. . . ."

She saw Josh and Jake nudge each other and smirk. She stopped reciting, but not for that reason. "I'm sorry, but that's all I memorized," she said. "It's a really long poem."

"Why, Caroline, we've got that in a book," said Mrs. Hatford. "It belonged to my grandmother. Let me find it for you."

She walked across the room and reached high on a shelf for the book of poetry. Caroline was pleased that none of the boys groaned. They might have been making fun of her because of her name, but down deep, Caroline felt sure they were enjoying her performance.

So she continued reading the poem about a lonely man grieving for his lost love, Lenore, and when he went to the door to see who was tapping, he found "Darkness there and nothing more." But the tapping continued, and just as Caroline read the line " 'Tis the wind and nothing more," there actually did come a *tap, tap, tap*ping at the back door of the Hatford house. Everyone jumped.

"A ghost!" said Peter.

"I think maybe we imagined it, Caroline is reading so well," said Mrs. Hatford.

But no, it came again, and—taking the lantern—Mr. Hatford went to answer. It was the next-door neighbor, asking if she could borrow a flashlight until the power came back on.

"Only that and nothing more," Mr. Hatford said, grinning, when he came back to join the circle.

Caroline went on. She felt she had never read so well, with such expression, in her entire life. When she came to the part where the man opened the shutter to the tapping, and in flew a raven, which "Perched, and sat, and nothing more," Peter listened with open mouth. And no matter how much the man tried to get the bird to tell him what it had come for or when it would leave, all the raven would say was "Nevermore."

"Quoth the Raven," Caroline said, and the others joined in the refrain: *"Nevermore."*

When she had finished at last, for the poem was several pages long, everyone clapped, and Caroline gave a little bow. And just as though she had performed in a theater, the power came back on. Lights blazed in every room, and the refrigerator began to hum.

"Oh, I'm so glad to see those lights," said Mrs. Hatford. "It wouldn't be easy getting this whole crew to bed in the dark."

"With that, I think *I'll* head for bed," said Mrs. Malloy. "I'm hoping that perhaps they'll have some power back on in Ohio tomorrow too. Maybe the storm broke the heat wave there." She went upstairs and into the bathroom.

Caroline wanted to linger, for an actress always liked people to come up after a performance and tell her how well she'd done. Indeed, both Mr. and Mrs. Hatford congratulated her on her expressiveness and interpretation of the poem.

Beth went on upstairs too, and it was only a few seconds later that Caroline saw the light come on in the girls' bedroom and heard her sister scream.

■ ■ ■ ■ ■ ■ ■ ■ ■ ■ ■ ■

Eighteen

■

Ka-boom!

Wally had started up the stairs when the second scream came, this time from Caroline. He couldn't imagine what the girls could be screaming about, unless someone had been found murdered on the floor.

The next voice he heard was Mrs. Malloy's. "Girls, now stop!"

Wally reached the doorway first, his family close at his heels. The girls and their mother were staring at the ceiling, so Wally looked up too. There were dozens and dozens of ladybugs. The ceiling looked like it had measles.

"*Now* what?" said Mr. Hatford.

"Oh, no!" said Wally's mother. "I've seen a few in the last couple of days, but *this* is an invasion!"

"What else?" said Jake, grinning at Josh. "*Lady*bugs, girls. Get it?"

A ladybug dropped from the ceiling and landed on

Caroline's arm. She screamed again, and when another landed on the back of her neck, she shrieked and jumped up and down.

Jake and Josh started to laugh, but Wally was fascinated by the ladybugs.

"The weather must have done it," said Mr. Hatford. "But how they're coming in, I don't know. Through the attic, maybe."

"Get the flyswatter," said Mrs. Hatford.

"Never mind the swatter," said her husband. "Get the vacuum cleaner."

With the Hatford boys and the Malloy girls watching from below, Mr. Hatford climbed up on a step stool, and holding the wand of the vacuum in one hand, he ran it over the ceiling.

Zing, zing, zing went the vacuum as one ladybug after another—sometimes three or four at a time—was sucked into the machine.

"I'm so sorry all this is happening while we're here," Mrs. Malloy said. "As though you needed one more thing!"

"The ladybugs would have come whether you were here or not, Jean," Mrs. Hatford said. "But they can really be a pain."

"Tell you what, Peter," his father said. "I'll give you a nickel for every dozen ladybugs you can catch. Take them out in the woods and let them go—whatever. But keep them away from the house."

Peter immediately started cupping his hands over the ones he found on the wall.

Caroline was sobbing. "I don't want to sleep in here,

Mother," she wailed. "They'll get in my hair and crawl in my pajamas."

Wally laughed out loud. He couldn't help it.

"Never mind her," Mrs. Malloy said quickly. "Caroline, we are lucky to have a roof over our heads, the fix we're in. Ladybugs aren't going to hurt you one bit." But Caroline went on weeping, and the vacuum went on sucking up bugs, and Peter kept trying to catch some and put them in a jar. Wally thought this was one of the best evenings he'd ever seen.

■

Mr. Malloy called from Ohio later, and after Mrs. Malloy had talked with him, she told the others that the electricity still had not come on in their house, but that the power company expected to have power restored to everyone in two more days.

"They are trying to restore electricity to nursing homes and hospitals first," she explained. "Houses, I guess, will be last on the list."

"We're glad to be able to do this for you, Jean. Stop worrying," Mrs. Hatford told her.

The heat wave broke the next day in West Virginia. Temperatures dropped from the hundreds to the eighties, and Wally knew that if he tried to fry an egg on the sidewalk now, it would sit there undisturbed all day.

Everyone felt better now that the air was more bearable, and Wally was determined to be as kind as he could to the girls for the last days they were there. When he went to breakfast, however, and saw Caroline with her hair plastered to her head like an onion skin, he stared, impolite or not.

"She tied a scarf around her head all night," Beth explained, trying not to laugh. But Wally and Jake and Josh and even Peter giggled in spite of themselves.

With the thought that the Malloys would be leaving soon, everybody seemed more relaxed. Beth made a double batch of chocolate chip cookies for Peter and his brothers. Mrs. Malloy drove to a market for sweet corn, and Caroline and Eddie picked tomatoes and green beans for dinner from Mrs. Hatford's garden.

Everyone seemed to be in a good mood at dinner. Mr. Hatford had finished his rounds early, Mrs. Hatford had been pleased to find dinner cooking when she came home from the hardware store, Peter had been busy collecting more ladybugs, and Jake and Eddie had sat down and played cards without any bickering.

"Now, this is what a summer evening should feel like!" Mr. Hatford said, reaching for another ear of corn, and at that exact moment there was a huge *Kaboom* that shook the house.

Wally almost leaped out of his skin. Peter dropped his fork, and several voices at once cried, "What was *that*?"

Because Tom Hatford was a part-time sheriff's deputy, he had a two-way radio, and immediately he leaped to his feet and rushed to turn it on. He stood in the doorway between the kitchen and the dining room, listening to the static and the excited voices and confusion coming from the speaker.

"Ray? . . . Ray?" Mr. Hatford kept saying. "What have we got? What exploded?"

And finally an answer: "I don't know, Tom. Larry says he sees smoke coming from east of town, and we've got a car on the way. . . . Wait a minute! It's the coal mine, Larry says. Son of a gun, we got a call coming in saying there's been an explosion at the old coal mine!"

Wally stared at his brothers, then at the girls.

"Why would anyone have done *that*?" Mrs. Hatford said. "Why, nobody's used that mine for years!"

"*Who* would do it—that's what we want to know," said Mr. Hatford, grabbing his keys and rushing for the door.

■

The peach cobbler that Mrs. Malloy had made for dinner sat untouched on the kitchen counter.

"Well, it's not end of the world," Mrs. Hatford said, puzzled. "As far as the sheriff and the police can tell, no one was hurt. Come and eat your dessert and we'll know more about the mine when Tom comes back."

"I'm not very hungry," said Wally, getting up from the table.

"Me neither," said Eddie. "Maybe I'll have some later."

Caroline and Beth and Jake and Josh left the kitchen too, and only Peter stayed in his chair, heaping on the ice cream and spooning the warm peaches and cream and crust into his mouth.

"*Now* what, Ellen?" said Mrs. Malloy. "You'd think *they* were the ones who blew up the mine."

Out on the porch, Wally said, "The shopping list!"

"Right!" said Jake. "We've got to show it to Dad! Where is it?"

"I don't know!" said Wally. He thrust his hand into his right pocket. Nothing there. He stuck both hands into both pockets and searched around with his fingers. Nothing.

"What were you wearing the day you found it?" asked Jake. "*Think,* Wally!"

"My other pants," Wally said. "I was wearing shorts, I guess. They were in the hamper, and Mom's washing clothes tomorrow!" Wally made a beeline for the basement stairs, Caroline and her sisters following, Jake and Josh at their heels.

"What's going on?" asked Mrs. Hatford as they crossed the kitchen.

"Nothing," said Wally.

They thundered down the basement stairs and over to the heaping baskets of dirty clothes by the washing machine. The boys tore through the clothes, sending shirts and towels flying this way and that, until finally Wally held up the wrinkled shorts he'd been wearing for the past week. He dug in the pockets. Success! He held up the worn slip of paper triumphantly and read, " 'Eggs, Rope, Tomato sauce, Flashlight, Dynamite.' "

"First-class evidence!" said Jake.

"Not quite," said Eddie.

"Why not?" asked Josh.

Eddie pointed. There on the stand next to the washing machine were a bottle of bleach, a bag of clothespins, and a large blue container of detergent. The red and yellow label said, DYNAMITE! FOR ALL YOUR WASHDAY NEEDS.

■

It was about nine-thirty when Tom Hatford came back, his clothes dusty.

"Well," he said. "All we can tell is that some person—or persons—set a charge at the entrance to the old mine and sealed it up. What we *won't* know until we get a crew out there tomorrow to haul some rock away is whether there was anybody in there."

Wally hadn't even thought of that.

"You mean, it might be *murder*?" he asked.

"All I'm saying is that somebody had a reason to close up the entrance to that tunnel. And we won't know the reason till we find out who did it. We're checking with every explosives place around here to see who they've sold to in the last week or month. We asked the residents out near the mine if they'd noticed anything out of the ordinary. People go back there from time to time to fish the river or climb the rocks. They dump some old tires, maybe, or a broken stove." He stopped suddenly, facing the row of kids sitting on the sofa.

"You know," he said, "you guys don't look so good. A little green around the gills, if you ask me. Do *you* know anything that might give us a clue?"

124

Peter came out of the kitchen holding his second bowl of peach cobbler, licking the back of the spoon. Jake gave him a warning look, and Peter said softly, "I won't tell!"

Wally's heart sank.

"Tell what, Peter?" asked his father.

"What I'm not supposed to," said Peter.

■ ■ ■ ■ ■ ■ ■ ■ ■ ■ ■ ■

Nineteen

■

Tippy

"**W**ell, whatever you're not supposed to tell me is exactly what I want to hear, so let's hear it," Mr. Hatford said firmly.

Peter stared down at his bowl.

"Who was up there? Somebody we know?" his father asked.

"A man," Peter said, his lips scarcely moving.

"*Who?*"

"I don't know. A man in a truck."

"When did you see him?"

"A couple days ago."

Caroline closed her eyes momentarily. They were all going to prison; she was sure of it. They had all been up to a place they weren't supposed to be. She imagined herself in jail wearing a black and white striped suit. Or maybe it was orange.

"What was the man doing?" Mr. Hatford asked Peter.

"Chasing."

The two mothers were in the doorway now, and Mr. Hatford remained standing, hands on his hips, facing the row of six kids squeezed together on the couch.

"Who was the man chasing, Peter?" asked his mother.

"I can't tell," said Peter. "I promised."

"If you don't tell, Peter, the wrong person may be blamed for that explosion. If you want to help the police do their work, you'd better tell me," said his father. "In fact, if you want to eat at the table for the next week, you'd better tell me *now*! Who was he chasing?"

Peter looked helplessly at Jake, then back down at his peach cobbler. "Us," he said in a tiny voice. "Well, not all of us, exactly. He was chasing Eddie and Jake."

"*Why?*"

"Because . . . because they climbed through the fence."

There were two or three seconds of silence, and then came another explosion, this time right there in the room as Mr. Hatford's voice filled every centimeter of space.

"Don't you two know better than to do that?" he bellowed. "You're the oldest of the bunch and you go set an example like that?" He turned on Jake. "How many times have I told you boys never, ever to go near that mine? Are you numskulls?"

And now Mrs. Malloy's voice was loud. "Eddie,

127

what were you *doing* up there? How *could* you do something so dangerous?"

"We . . . we just wanted to see what was in the tunnel. We weren't going to go down a shaft or anything," Eddie said meekly.

"It was a dare," Jake explained uncomfortably. "I dared Eddie to do it and she dared me."

"That's the stupidest reason I can think of!" Mr. Hatford continued yelling. "Dumb, dumb, dumb! I thought you two were smarter than that."

"I'm sorry," mumbled Jake, staring down at his hands.

"So who *was* this man?" asked his father.

"I don't know," Jake answered. "All of a sudden, there he was, going all crazy, and we tore out of there."

"He didn't have on a uniform or anything," said Eddie. "I don't think he was a guard."

"We just went tearing down the hill as fast as we could with him yelling at us never to come back," said Jake.

"Do you realize what a dangerous thing you kids have done?" Mr. Hatford boomed. "If he was the one who set off that charge, do you realize he might have been going to set the explosives off that very day you were up there?" He stared at them some more and shook his head in disgust. "You kids sit right there and don't move while I call the sheriff. I'm going to let him question you."

■

The adults were talking in the kitchen. The seven kids sat in the living room, Peter looking most miserable of all.

"Man oh man, are we in for it!" said Josh. "I've never seen Dad so mad."

"I have!" said Peter brightly, wanting to redeem himself. "Remember the time Jake called the termite inspector to go to the house next door and—"

"Shut up," said Jake.

The more Caroline thought about it, the more relieved she was that her own father wasn't there. With both of the dads yelling, it would have been like thunder in the house.

There was the sound of a car pulling into the driveway, then footsteps and voices on the porch. Mrs. Hatford answered the door, and both the sheriff and the chief of police walked in. Mr. Hatford pointed out Jake and Eddie. The sheriff sat down.

Caroline listened while Jake had to explain all over again how he and Eddie had sort of dared each other to go into the old coal mine—how they hadn't intended to go down a shaft; they'd just wanted to peek, to say that they'd gone in. And the way he told it, it sounded as though he and Eddie were longtime friends.

"Your dad says a man at the mine chased you," the police chief said. "Where did he come from?"

"We don't know!" said Jake. "He seemed to pop up out of nowhere."

"Was he in the tunnel or outside it?"

"Outside," said Caroline. "I think he was in the bushes."

"As soon as we heard him shouting, we ran," said Eddie. "We'd only just stepped inside the entrance when we heard him."

"How tall was he?" asked the sheriff. "Tall as I am?"

"Shorter, maybe," said Jake.

"Taller!" said Wally. "I saw him chasing you and he looked like a giant to me!"

"He was not!" said Beth.

The sheriff rolled his eyes. "Okay, what did he look like? Did he have a beard? A mustache?"

"Yes," said Caroline. "A beard. I think."

"He didn't have a beard!" said Josh. "I'd remember if he had a beard."

"He had a mustache, but he didn't have a beard," said Beth.

"What color was his hair?" asked the chief of police.

"Gray," said Josh.

"Yellow," said Jake. "A yellowish color."

"Brown," said Caroline.

"We don't even know what color his hair was. He was wearing a cap," said Wally.

"Can't you kids agree on *any*thing?" asked the police chief.

"He was driving a truck!" said Peter. "We all saw that. An old rusty truck."

"Yes!" said Caroline. "An old rusty brown truck."

"Did anyone get the license number?" asked the sheriff.

The kids hung their heads.

"Was it a West Virginia license plate, at least? Can you tell us that?" asked the sheriff.

"I think so," said Josh.

"But you're not sure. Did anyone actually *see* the license plate?"

Nobody had.

"And that was the last you saw of him and his truck?" asked the police chief.

"No, he was outside our house on the road," said Caroline.

"Here?" cried Mrs. Hatford.

"Did you get a good look at him?" asked the sheriff.

Josh shook his head. "We were underwater," he said. "I mean, when we saw him stop his truck, we ducked down under the water."

"We didn't want him to know who we were," said Caroline.

"Did he say anything to you?"

"No," she said. "Just looked at us, then drove away. It was creepy."

The sheriff was writing things down on a notepad, and for a while Caroline figured he had asked every question there was to ask. Surely by now he knew that she and her sisters and the Hatford boys had nothing to do with that explosion.

The sheriff closed his notebook. He put his pen back in his pocket. And then, just when Caroline thought the worst was over, he leaned forward, looked from one kid to the next until his eyes had traveled down the whole row, and said, "Who's Tippy?"

■ ■ ■ ■ ■ ■ ■ ■ ■ ■ ■ ■

Twenty

■

E-mail to Georgia

Dear Bill (and Danny and Steve and Tony and Doug):

I don't know if your computer is hooked up. For all I know, you guys could already be on your way back here. But man oh man, have you ever missed some excitement!

First, you won't believe this, but the Malloys have been staying here for the past few days because there's a heat wave in Ohio and all their electricity is off. They'd already left your house when they found out, and all their furniture was gone, so Mom invited them to stay with us till the power came back on. They've been sleeping in Jake and Josh's bedroom, all four of them. Talk about weird!

And they threw our underwear in the closet! You know what would be even worse? If the heat wave hadn't broken here in West Virginia, our power went out, and we had to go to Ohio and stay in their house for a while. That would be so awful I don't even want to think about it.

Then a storm came up here and the heat wave broke and we were without power for a while. Then we had a ladybug invasion and Caroline freaked out. Dad's been paying Peter a nickel for every dozen he collects, and he's already got a jarful.

That's just for starters.

Then . . . Jake and Eddie dared each other to go to the old coal mine. They've really been bugging each other. It's like having a cat and a dog under the same roof, and we've all been getting a little sick of them. Anyway, they did go, and a man came charging out of nowhere, yelling at them to get out. Two days ago there was a big explosion at the entrance to the mine. Peter, of course, told Dad we'd been there, and Dad called the sheriff and the chief of police. They came over and asked us a lot of questions.

And you know who did it? Who set off the dynamite? The guy who was yelling at us at the mine. And you know who he was? Some old man whose dog Tippy fell in that mine shaft and died down there and the guy didn't discover where he was till too late. He told the police he'd been looking for his dog for a long time and finally found where he'd fallen in. The guy was so mad that the county hadn't closed up that mine, and so worried, I guess, that some kid might fall in there someday——especially when he saw Jake and Eddie in there——that he figured he'd better do something about it himself, so he bought some dynamite and blew up the entrance. Then he took a sharp rock and scratched something on the rocky wall: *This is for you, Tippy.*

That was how the police found him. That, and our description of his truck. I don't know what will happen to him. The newspaper says he did the county a service—the old coal mine should have been sealed up decades ago, and this guy did it for us. But the police say you can't go around setting off explosives no matter how good your reason might be. Dad thinks the guy will probably have to pay a fine, but that's all. And the newspaper might even pay it for him, for doing a public service!

But you guys should have been here! It was a blast, in more ways than one. Right in the middle of the police chief's questioning us, a ladybug landed on Caroline's shoulder—they're still coming into the house from somewhere—and she jumped up and down and screamed. Now even the chief of police knows she's nuts.

The girls will probably be going back to Ohio tomorrow. That's when their power's supposed to come back on, according to their dad. If you don't get here soon, there won't be any time left before school starts again. If you get this e-mail, write back.

Wally (and Jake and Josh and Peter)

Twenty-one

■

E-mail from Georgia

Dear Wally (and Jake and Josh and Peter):

Hey, man! You guys really do get the excitement, don't you?

You know what I wish? I wish we had stayed in Buckman while the girls were there. I mean, I wish they'd been living someplace else and we could have been in on all the jokes and stuff.

All the summer sports are over down here, and we'll be leaving for Buckman tomorrow. Dad plans to drive straight through in one day, so we have to get up at five in the morning. This is the last time we can use the computer before it's packed. I sure hope our house is still the way we left it. I hope the girls haven't put ballerina wallpaper in our bedrooms. I hope that Buckman is just the way we remember it, and that the swinging bridge hasn't been washed away in a storm or anything.

What was it you always called those girls—the Whomper, the Weirdo, and the Crazie? Eddie the Whomper, because she could hit a baseball so far; Beth the Weirdo, because she read all those gross books about aliens and stuff; and Caroline the Crazie, because you never knew what she'd do next. Tell the Whomper, the Weirdo, and the Crazie goodbye for us. Tell them we'd better not find any weird stuff in our rooms. Tell them this time when they go back to Ohio, stay there. And if they can't stay there, then at least come back when we're around to help make their lives miserable.

Bill (and Tony and Danny and Steve and Doug)

Twenty-two

■

Goodbye! Goodbye!

The call came at seven-thirty the following night. The electricity was on again in Ohio.

"Hooray!" shouted Eddie and Beth and Caroline together, and Mrs. Malloy's face relaxed with relief and pleasure.

"We're going to leave first thing in the morning," she told the Hatfords. "You have all been so wonderful to put up with us for five days."

"It's been wonderful for me to come home and find dinner all prepared and the house straightened up," said Mrs. Hatford. "And it gave us a chance to get to know each other a little better, Jean."

"Are we really, truly leaving, Mom?" asked Caroline.

"Right after breakfast," her mother answered. "I want you girls to pack up all your things tonight and set your bags out in the hall, ready to go. Then all you'll need to do in the morning is put your pajamas and toothbrushes in your bags, and we're off."

The girls did the dishes and cleared the table that evening. As soon as they were done, while the boys were watching a preseason football game on TV, Eddie whispered to her sisters, "We've got to pay a visit to the Benson place before we go."

"How can we?" Beth asked. "The house is all cleaned up and locked, Eddie. Mom's already left the key with Mrs. Hatford."

"We don't need a key," said Eddie. "Just follow me."

Were they going to get in trouble again just before they left? Caroline wondered. Hadn't their trip to the old coal mine been trouble enough?

"If we do something bad, Eddie, God will probably turn off the electricity in Ohio again, and we'll have to stay here forever," she said.

"God wouldn't punish the whole state of Ohio just because of us," Eddie told her. "Get a flashlight and let's go."

Out the back door they went, being careful not to let the screen slam. They went down the steps, around the side of the house, and across the road, then started across the swinging bridge to the other side of the river.

"I'm going to be sorry to leave all this," said Caroline in a small voice.

And she was surprised to hear Eddie say, "Me too. Ohio's going to seem so boring without the boys."

"There are boys in Ohio, too," said Beth, "but not as nice as Josh Hatford."

138

"So what are we doing going back to the old Benson place?" asked Caroline.

"Just a little something to make sure they don't forget us," said Eddie.

Up the hill they went until they could see the house and the old barn that was used for a garage.

"Into the garage," said Eddie.

And once inside, she said, "Up the ladder."

They had a lot of good memories of the loft in the old Benson barn. Who could forget the "abaguchie" they trapped in the barn, with Wally up in the loft? Or the way the girls had spied on the boys from the loft window and vice versa?

"What do we do now?" asked Beth when all three of them were on the floor above.

In answer, Eddie pulled out her Swiss Army knife and tried it out on one of the wooden rafters. It made a deep clean cut. "I just want to make sure they remember our names," she said. "Hold the flashlight, Beth."

Caroline clapped her hands delightedly. "Be sure to include my middle name," she said.

The Malloys were here, Eddie carved, making slow deep cuts in the wood. *Eddie, Beth, and Caroline Lenore.* Then she sat back on her heels to admire her work.

"The next time the Hatfords and the Bensons crawl up here for one of their club meetings, they'll have us to remember!" said Beth.

"As though they could ever forget *us*!" said Caroline,

taking the knife and carving an exclamation point after her name.

Eddie slipped the knife into her pocket, and the girls crawled back across the floor—through old screen doors and boxes of junk—to the ladder. Caroline went down first and walked over to the door. But when she tried to push it open, it wouldn't budge.

"Hey!" she yelled. "Someone's locked us in!"

"What?" said Eddie.

"The door won't move," said Caroline, pushing with all her strength.

"But there wasn't any lock on that door!" said Eddie. "How could we be locked in?"

"We'll be here forever!" Caroline wailed dramatically. "No one knows we're over here, and the Bensons aren't back!"

"*Can* it, Caroline!" Eddie said. "Save your tears for Broadway." And then she whispered, "I'll bet the Hatfords are right outside holding the door closed."

She and Beth and Caroline all put their shoulders against the door and pushed. It gave a little but bounced back. There was muffled laughter from the other side.

Eddie leaned over and whispered something into Caroline's ear, and immediately Caroline began to smile. While Eddie and Beth kept pushing against the door, Caroline climbed back up the ladder and crawled over to the loft window, dragging a box of old hubcaps with her.

She peered out the window in the gathering dark,

and sure enough, there were Jake and Josh and Wally, all laughing, all pushing hard against the garage door.

Caroline lifted the box of hubcaps to the edge of the window. She held one out.

"Look out below!" she yelled.

Wally looked up. "Hey!" he yelled as the box began to tip. "She means it!"

The three boys scattered just before a rain of hubcaps tumbled down, rolling and clanking and clunking all over the ground.

Eddie and Beth burst through the door, and they all ended up laughing as they ran after the rolling hubcaps and got them back in the box and up to the loft again.

As they walked together back down the hill to the swinging bridge, the moon full in the sky, a light breeze blowing, Caroline said to herself, *Always remember this moment, because it will never come again.* Caroline was full of "last moments," because they always seemed so dramatic, something she could remember when she went onstage.

■

The girls packed up as their mother had said to, and set their bags outside the bedroom door. The next morning, Mrs. Malloy woke them early so that they could have breakfast with the Hatfords. The boys were sitting sleepy-eyed over their cereal at the table, and Mr. Hatford had on his postal uniform, ready to leave for work.

"I'm going to miss finding you here when I get home from work each day," Mrs. Hatford told them.

"It was nice having girls around the house for a change." She ignored the groans from the boys.

"But you won't miss having four extra people lined up for the bathroom, and clothes all over the place," Mrs. Malloy told her. "Now you can have your house back the way it was, and I can't tell you how grateful I am that you let us stay."

Mr. Hatford carried their bags and suitcases out to the car before he told them goodbye. Then he got in his own car and drove off. The girls stood facing the boys on the driveway, all of them feeling awkward and wishing the moment was over.

"Goodbye, Ellen. You're a jewel," Mrs. Malloy said, hugging the boys' mother.

"Goodbye, Jean. Have a safe trip," said Mrs. Hatford.

There was no hugging the boys, of course—except Peter. Each girl hugged him hard.

"I don't want you to go," he said in his little-boy voice.

"Well, you still have some of those cookies we baked," Beth said. "I put extra chocolate chips in them, just for you."

Eddie looked at the boys. "Goodbye, guys. Have a crummy year," she said, laughing.

"Goodbye," said Jake, grinning. "Hope you flunk seventh grade."

The mothers looked helplessly at each other. "Where did we fail?" Mrs. Malloy said, laughing.

"Goodbye, Wally," said Caroline. "Look for my name on Broadway."

"Sure, when the Mississippi River runs dry," said Wally.

The girls climbed into the car, and Mrs. Malloy got into the driver's seat.

"All we need now is for the car not to start and to have to spend another week with the Hatfords while it's fixed," said Beth.

But the car did start, and soon it was backing down the drive. The girls waved. The boys waved. Caroline pressed her nose against the window and watched as the boys disappeared, the house disappeared, and the swinging bridge disappeared. In just a few minutes, she and her mother and sisters were out of town.

■

"Okay, boys," Mrs. Hatford said. "Go back upstairs and air out your sleeping bags. Pick up all your clothes and put them either back in your drawers or in the hamper."

The boys usually hated the job of straightening up, but Wally was so eager to get his room all to himself again, and the twins were so eager to get their own bedroom back, that they went straight upstairs to gather their stuff.

Jake and Josh took their sleeping bags out on the back porch and unzipped them, then flopped them over the railing.

"Hey!" yelped Jake. "There are ladybugs in mine!"

"Mine too!" cried Josh as bugs began flying in all directions.

Two notes fluttered to the ground, one from each

bag. Wally, who had heard the twins' yells, came running out on the steps and picked one up.

" 'A little something to remember us by,' " he read aloud.

Josh read the other: " 'The Whomper, the Weirdo, and the Crazie.' "

■

"Caroline, will you please stop wailing!" said her mother from the driver's seat. "I can't listen to that all the way to Ohio."

"Yeah, Caroline, get a grip," said Eddie.

"This was the most exciting year of my life and it will never come again," Caroline said, weeping. "We didn't even get their e-mail addresses. We may never hear from them again."

"That would be so bad?" said Eddie.

"We can always call, you know," said Beth.

Caroline unzipped her backpack and pulled out a tissue to blow her nose. Then she screamed.

"*Now* what?" said her mother.

"Ladybugs!" cried Caroline. "My backpack's full of them! And here's a note!"

Beth snatched it from her hand and read it to the others: " 'Thought you'd like something from Buckman to take along with you. Have a good trip. Jake and Josh, Wally and Peter.' "

■

Now, you tell me: who won the war?

must interview each other for the dreaded December class project. Caroline, as usual, has a trick up her sleeve that's sure to shock Wally. In the meantime, Wally and his brothers find a way to spy on the Malloy girls at home. The girls vow to get revenge on those sneaky Hatfords with a trap the boys won't soon forget.

A Traitor Among the Boys

The Hatford boys make a New Year's resolution to treat the Malloy girls like sisters. But who says you can't play tricks on sisters? The girls will need to stay one step ahead of the boys and are willing to pay big-time for advance information. Homemade cookies should be all it takes to make a traitor spill the beans. In the meantime, Caroline is delighted with her role in the town play. Don't ask how Beth, Josh, and Wally get roped into it—just wait until showtime, when Caroline pulls her wildest stunt yet!

A Spy Among the Girls

Valentine's Day is coming up, and love is in the air for Beth Malloy and Josh Hatford. When they're spotted holding hands, Josh tells his teasing brothers that he's simply spying on the girls to see what they're plotting next. At the same time, Caroline Malloy, the family actress, decides she must know what it's like to fall in love. Poor Wally Hatford is in for it when she chooses him as the object of her affection!

The Boys Return

It's spring break, and the only assignment Wally Hatford and Caroline Malloy have is to do something they've never done before. Wally's sure that will be a cinch, because the mighty Benson brothers are coming. It will be nonstop action all the way. For starters, the nine Benson and Hatford boys plan to scare the three Malloy sisters silly by convincing them that their house is haunted. Meanwhile, everyone in town has heard that there's a hungry cougar on the prowl. When the kids decide to take a break from their tricks and join forces to catch the cougar, guess who gets stuck with the scariest job?

The Girls Take Over

The Hatford boys and the Malloy girls are ready to outdo each other again. Eddie is the first girl ever to try out for the school baseball team. Now she and Jake are vying for the same position, while Caroline and Wally compete to become class spelling champ. As if that's not enough, the kids decide to race bottles down the rising Buckman River to see whose will travel farthest by the end of the month. Of course, neither team trusts the other, and when the girls go down to the river to capture the boys' bottles, well . . . it looks as if those Malloy girls may be in over their heads this time!

Boys in Control

Wally Hatford always seems to get a raw deal. The rest of the family goes to the ball game, and he has to stay home to watch over a yard sale. Caroline Malloy writes a silly play for a school project, and he gets roped into costarring in it with her! Things are looking down, especially when the Malloy girls stumble across an embarrassing item from the boys' past. But Wally finally gets his chance to turn the tables on the girls' scheme and prove who's really in control. Boys rule!

Girls Rule!

The rivalry between the Malloy sisters and the Hatford boys is heating up! The kids have two weeks to earn money for a fund-raising contest. All those who collect twenty dollars or more for the new children's wing at the hospital can be in the annual Strawberry Festival Parade or get lots of strawberry treats. The only place Caroline wants to be is on the Strawberry Queen's float. How will she earn the money in time? Do the Hatfords have moneymaking secrets they're not telling the girls?

Boys Rock!

Wally Hatford dreams of long, lazy days far away from school and Caroline Malloy. But Wally, the best speller among the Hatford brothers, gets roped into helping them with a summer newspaper project that will earn the twins school credit. What does that get Wally? When he hears scratching noises coming from Oldakers' bookstore cellar, Mr. Oldaker trusts him to keep a secret that could turn into a scoop for their newspaper. Wally worries that the secret may be too scary to keep to himself. What's worse, the Malloy girls have horned in on the newspaper. If there's one person Wally won't spill his secret to, it's nutty Caroline Malloy!